PROFIT FOR THE PICAROON

John Cassells

PROFIT FOR
THE PICAROON

JOHN LONG, LONDON

JOHN LONG LIMITED
3 Fitzroy Square, London W1

AN IMPRINT OF THE  HUTCHINSON GROUP

London Melbourne Sydney Auckland
Wellington Johannesburg Cape Town
and agencies throughout the world

First published 1972

*This book has been set in Pilgrim type, printed
in Great Britain by Anchor Press, and
bound by Wm. Brendon, both of Tiptree, Essex*

ISBN 0 09 109870 X

1

It was Herodotus who declared, a very long time ago indeed, that accidents rule men, not men accidents. It was Schopenhauer who demonstrated that a man must wait for the right moment. It was Ludovic Saxon, otherwise the Picaroon, who gave point to the fact that, if a man combined these aphorisms, both philosophers might be proven to have something on the ball, and that with a bit of luck and good management there might be a fair measure of gain all round.

As to the accident itself. It occurred on a secondary road a few miles south of Lambourn, when the Simca, driven by a blonde and very attractive young lady, came out of a side road, the entrance to which was obscured by bushes, and compelled the Jaguar, driven by the Picaroon, to swing to the right, mount the raised edge and crash through a wooden fence, to strand itself in a field of turnips.

The Picaroon opened his eyes to find his head cradled against a soft thigh, and to look up and into pale and pretty features which were very close indeed to his own. Her eyes were cornflower blue, her hair was ash blonde and silken and he was vaguely aware that long cool fingers were stroking his brow very gently. He closed his eyes tightly again. It was of an afternoon in early June. The air was balmy and mellow, hushed but for the humming bees, and the pleasant murmurings of pigeons in the tree tops, and through this vaguely entrancing silence Ludovic Saxon heard a voice which might, quite easily, have belonged to one of the well known *houris* of paradise say:

'Are you all right?'

The Picaroon lay for a moment or so in what was possibly the nearest proximination to heaven he was likely to find himself, then cautiously opened one eye. He heard the girl draw in her breath.

'Can you hear me?' She stroked his forehead again.

Ludovic groaned. He hoped it was a realistic groan.

She slid her hand under his lightweight jacket and explored his ribs.

The Picaroon giggled and the hand was hastily withdrawn.

'Ticklish,' he said.

'I was trying to find if you had any ribs broken.'

Ludovic sighed and eased himself up a little. He made a cautious survey. 'No ribs broken.' He moved his limbs. 'No legs either.' He looked at her with satisfaction. 'So far as I can see, I'm intact.'

She wriggled away from him a little. 'Thank goodness for that. You gave me a hideous fright.' She leaned across with a handkerchief and touched his head gently. 'You've cut your scalp though. It's bleeding quite a lot.'

'Vascular,' Ludovic said. 'I know it of old. This scalp of which you speak, young lady, has had its own experiences in life. If I told you what it had gone through, the chances are you wouldn't believe me.' He groped in his pocket, produced a packet of cigarettes and held it towards her.

She shook her head. 'No thank you. I don't smoke.'

'I do,' Ludovic said. He lit one, flicked his lighter flame and sat upright the better to survey her.

She was indeed astonishingly pretty. Twenty or twenty-one, fair, and wearing a blue linen frock. Now

6

that her colour had returned, she looked healthily tanned, crisp, fresh as a morning lettuce, but more than a little apprehensive.

The Picaroon smoked in silence for a moment or two, then: 'I suppose we'd better have a look and see what the damage is.'

'I suppose so.' She drew a deep breath. 'Thank goodness you're not badly hurt. It gave me a horrible fright.'

'I'll bet it did.'

'When I saw you leave the road and go through the hedge, I thought you'd be killed.'

The Picaroon considered. He looked across towards the stranded Jaguar. 'How did you get me out?'

'The door opened and you were thrown out.' She rose a little shakily. 'Someone is coming now. Good, it's Capper. He's the postman.'

A red postal van had drawn up forty or fifty yards away and a man in the uniform of a postman was stepping through the gap in the hedge towards them. He raised a hand towards his cap. 'Anyone hurt, Miss Sheldon?

'This gentleman here. He was thrown out of his car.'

The Picaroon struggled up, stiffly. 'I think I'm all right.' He began to walk up and down cautiously. 'So far as I can gather everything's functioning.'

Capper said, 'That's good, sir. Not much use in asking how it happened. It's a bad concealed entrance that if you don't know it. I been waiting for something to happen there for long enough. Always watch it, myself.' He looked at the girl. 'You're all right, miss?'

'Yes, I got a fright. That was all. But could you help this gentleman down to the road, Capper, and we'll get him into my car? I'll take him up to the house.'

The Picaroon made noises of protest.

She overrode him crisply. 'Of course you'll come up to the house. We'd better have Dr. Platt over to see you and Daddy is certainly going to want to hear about your

7

accident.' She put her arm around his waist. 'Lean on me and Capper and we'll get you over to the car.'

The Picaroon was faintly amused. A moment or so later, he found himself in the rear of the Simca with Capper nodding to him sympathetically.

'You'll be all right there, sir. Miss Sheldon can manage you fine and the commander will give you a hand at the house. I'm going into Hillmeet now. I'll stop at the garage and have Denton come up with the rhino and pull you out of there. I don't think there's any harm done to your car, but Denton will look it over for you.' He raised a hand in farewell. 'Got to get along now or I'll be late with the Hillmeet lift.' He went back to the little red van.

The girl touched the starter. 'Well, that's that. End of a bright afternoon.' She looked round at him. 'You're sure you're not hurt?'

'Positive.'

'What about shock?'

'It takes a lot to shock me.

She surveyed him critically. 'I can believe that. Now, before we go up to the house, I'm Mally Sheldon.'

'And my name is Saxon. Ludovic Saxon.'

She looked at him quickly. 'Ludovic Saxon! I've heard of you.'

Most people have,' Ludovic said smugly.

'The Picaroon.'

'That's right.'

'I've heard a lot about you,' she went on, 'from Amantha Selby.'

'Adrian Selby's sister?'

'Yes.' She inspected him a little more critically. 'I'd never have recognised you, Mr. Saxon. Amantha said you were very good-looking.'

Ludovic was faintly annoyed. 'And what would you say?'

She brushed his query aside. 'Amantha said you helped

8

Adrian out when he was in a pretty awkward position.'

'I suppose that's true.'

'Amantha says—'

'I'm getting a bit fed up with what this Amantha says,' Ludovic said warmly. 'What I want now is a bit of a wash-up and a drink, and if—'

'Of course. I'm sorry, Mr. Saxon.'

'Ludovic,' he told her. 'All my friends call me Ludovic.'

'I don't know that I'm exactly a friend,' she said thoughtfully. 'If it hadn't been for me there would have been no accident at all. And while we're on the subject, I've got to think up a good way of presenting it to Daddy.'

'Daddy's going to create?'

'He certainly is. I've had a bit of trouble before. I've had my licence endorsed just because an absolute clown of a magistrate, who was so old he shouldn't have been on the bench at all, couldn't understand what I was trying to tell him in the plainest of English. You would imagine that they'd give these fairly responsible positions to people with a more incisive type of mind, but—'

'Things were ever thus,' the Picaroon agreed gloomily.

She started up the car and drove along the road in silence. It was a narrow, twisting, tree-lined road and after a few moments they swung through a wide gateway and up a slight rise towards a modest, but pleasant-looking country house. The drive swung round towards the front door, and the girl drew up in front of it.

'The Pines,' she said. 'In the distance, Daddy.'

The Picaroon saw a bulky figure in shirt sleeves prodding around him with a hoe. So far, he noted their approach had not been observed.

Mally made certain now that this state of affairs should not continue. She pressed on the horn with some vigour. 'Daddy's a little bit deaf.'

'But not so deaf he didn't hear that,' said the Picaroon.

9

This was true. Daddy was peering towards them. Now he tossed down the hoe, picked up his jacket and slung it over his shoulders. He began to walk towards them with a long and purposeful stride, and when he was close enough the Picaroon, who, in his day, had met a wide selection of Daddies, was able to see that this was one of the large economy size, with massive shoulders, great hairy forearms and an enormous expanse of pink chest which, for the afternoon sun was beating fiercely upon it, gave the impression that he was wearing a coat of mail, until he was close enough for the Picaroon to observe that this singular phenomenon was occasioned by no more than a luxurious crop of hair. He came towards them, peering at Ludovic and when he was twenty or thirty yards away called: 'What's all this? What's all this? Thought you were going to Lambourn?'

'I was, Daddy.'

'But you didn't go,' he said. 'You didn't go. What about my tobacco? What about the whisky from Paine and Findlay? That's what I want to know. You left here not twenty minutes ago to go to Lambourn, but you didn't go. Stands to reason, don't it?' He stared out of very blue sailor's eyes at the Picaroon. 'Who's this?'

'A friend of the Selbys, Daddy. You remember Adrian and Amantha. This is Mr. Saxon. My father, Commander Sheldon.'

The Picaroon found his hand engulfed in a vast pink paw. 'Saxon, eh? Used to be a Saxon on the old *Warspite* with me. "Sheep" we called him. Any friend of yours?'

The Picaroon denied kinship.

'Not that it matters,' said the commander. He pointed a finger at the girl. 'Where did you run into her?'

'I didn't,' Ludovic said. 'Very nearly though and—' Mally sighed. 'Daddy, there was an accident!'

'An accident!'

'At the road end,' she said.

'You ran into him?'

'No.'

'He ran into you?'

'No. It wasn't really so bad as all that. Mr. Saxon swerved to the right and went through the hedge into the turnip field. His car is there yet. We'll have to phone Denton and have him tow it into the village and—'

The commander left them abruptly to walk round the Simca. After a brisk but rigorous inspection he returned. 'No damage done that I can see, and that's a damn good thing, Mally. You know what I told you. One more accident and you'll use the legs God gave you instead of driving around in motor cars. Just one more.' He wiped perspiration from his forehead with the back of his hand, looked at them both and then nodded. 'Come on inside,' he said.

He led the way into the house.

2

The commander took him into a long cool room. 'Sit down, Saxon. Get you a drink. What's it to be? Gin, whisky?'

'Beer,' said the Picaroon.

Mally Sheldon took a hand. 'First of all, Daddy, Mr. Saxon's going to go up to the bathroom and tidy himself. He's covered with mud and blood and I'm not sure that he shouldn't have the doctor.'

'Better without him,' Sheldon said. 'Don't believe in doctors myself. Never consulted a doctor in my life. Had to go before boards and what not, mind you, in my service days, but no more than that. Never thought much of them at any time.'

The Picaroon also thought he could dispense with the services of the doctor, but he permitted himself to be led upstairs to a large, old-fashioned bathroom where towels were already laid out.

The girl turned on the taps. 'We've got plenty of hot water, Mr. Saxon.'

'Ludovic,' he said. 'I mentioned it before.'

'All right. Ludovic. A bath will take the stiffness out of your bones at any rate.'

The Picaroon was irritable. 'What makes you think I've got stiffness in my bones anyway? You would imagine I was positively ancient.'

'Amantha said—'

The Picaroon moved towards her. 'If I hear any more about this damned Amantha—'

She edged hurriedly towards the door. 'I'm sorry, Ludovic, but do have a good bath. I'm certain you'll feel better after it. When you're ready you know where to come.'

'I do,' Ludovic agreed, 'and the thought of beer makes me want to hurry. Be down in five minutes. You can practically pour it out for me now.'

In fact it was some quarter of an hour later that he made his way a shade stiffly down the old-fashioned stairway. He had been shaken up a little more than he cared to admit, but the warmth and comfort of the water had caressed away most of his stiffness. Now he made his way into the sitting-room, clean, glowing and redolent of coal tar soap, where the commander rose to greet him.

'Come in, my boy, and sit down. About this drink. I've been giving it some thought. Whisky's the thing for you.' He proceeded to pour out a large one, topped up his own while he was at it, and sat down. 'Well, a quick recovery.'

'Thank you, sir.' Ludovic took a mouthful.

The commander licked his lips. 'Not bad stuff, eh? Get it from a cousin of mine up in Scotland. Keep that blend for special occasions. This is a special occasion.' He lifted a large-bowled blackened pipe from a vast cut glass ashtray. 'Smoke up if you want to. Can I offer you a fill?' He drew over a tobacco jar.

The Picaroon shook his head. 'Cigarettes, I'm afraid, sir.' He lit one.

The commander struck a match. 'Never smoked but one in my life. Was at school at the time and I thought damned little of it. Bad for you, them things.' He looked around. 'Once or twice when she was younger I got Mally trying them out. Made her finish it off too, every time. That sickened her. Gone to make tea now. Be here in a minute or two. 'Phoning the garage and what not.'

She appeared a few moments later, wheeling a laden tea trolley. 'Good bath, Ludovic?'

'Excellent. I feel a bit better now.'

'I rang Denton,' she said. 'In fact it was his man I spoke to. Capper had already told him and he's on the way. He'll pull your car out and take it to the garage for a check up.'

'Good.'

'And now, will you have some tea?'

The Picaroon thought he would. 'Two lumps, and cream.' He reached for a sandwich. 'I feel I can do with it.'

'Tea!' the commander said. 'Never touch it. Coffee at breakfast, though I think damn little of that either. Still, a fellow has to drink something with his meals. Can't live on whisky all the time. Too damn dear. I can remember when it was only shillings for a bottle. That's what those damn Socialists did for us. Damn near six years of 'em and what did we have to show for it?

Whisky three pounds for a bottle and no more daylight saving time. That and all this new business of counting money.'

Mally poured out tea for the Picaroon. 'If you'd like to call anyone, Ludovic, the telephone is in the study.'

The Picaroon nodded. 'That's an idea. I'll call a friend and have him pick me up later in the evening. You don't mind that, sir?'

'Not a bit of it,' the commander said cheerfully. 'Stay as long as you like. Glad of someone to talk to, myself, and that's the truth of it. Damn all to do for me but hoe onions and I can think of things I'd rather do.' He poked the shank of his pipe in the Picaroon's direction. 'Should have retired to some sea coast place, that's what I should have done. I might have picked up a bit of a boat and messed about in it. Would have done it too if I hadn't had the place left me by an old uncle.'

'It's charming,' Ludovic said.

The older man nodded. 'I always liked it. Used to come here for holidays when I was a boy. Had some good times too, but, of course, all the people I knew then have gone.' He looked at the clock. 'Have to get out to those damned onions again.' He rose as he spoke. 'You take it easy, young feller. Could be you've had a bit of a shake. Sit around here and keep out of the sun. Drink in the cabinet there. Help yourself.' He stalked out.

Ludovic watched him go. 'I suppose he does feel it a bit quiet here after spending a lifetime in the Navy.'

'Not really. Daddy likes to complain. When he was in the Navy he was always wishing it was time to come out of it.' She rose. 'Do you want to use the telephone?'

'That's a good idea,' he told her. 'Lead me to it.'

She took him through to a small room which was equipped with a desk, two armchairs, a plain, wooden, swivel chair, and a series of photographs of naval craft and naval officers. 'This is Daddy's den. He comes in here to smoke and grouch. I don't come in much. That's the telephone. Make any calls you care to and come outside when you're through. I'll be in the garden.'

'First of all,' Ludovic said, 'this fellow Denton.'

'Hillmeet 323.' She closed the door behind her.

He dialled the number and spoke to Denton himself and the man was reassuring. There was little wrong with the car so far as Denton could see.

'Of course I haven't had a great deal of time to go over it, sir, but I'd say, if you had to, you could probably take her back to London tonight, though if I were in your place I'd prefer to wait till morning till I spend some on her. Bit of paintwork scraped off and there's a crack on the windscreen. Not a bad one, but it'll get worse. Engine's running a treat though.'

'I'll leave her for a day or so with you,' Ludovic said, and hung up. He lit a cigarette now and rang the flat in Courtfield Mews.

MacNab was at home and was considerably intrigued. 'An accident!' he said. 'There's a caper for you. Was there any damage done?'

'None at all. When can you come for me?'

MacNab pondered. 'I can make it by about eight or nine o'clock. I've got a wee bit of a job to attend to first, but there's no bother.'

'That should suit,' Ludovic said. 'Eight or nine o'clock then, Mac.'

In the event, MacNab arrived on the stroke of nine, and the Picaroon, replete with iced cucumber soup, Wye salmon, mayonnaise and new potatoes, salad and strawberries and cream, took a pleasant and grateful farewell.

'Come again,' the commander said. 'I enjoyed our little talk about the Red Sea. Did a bit of patrol work there, young feller me lad, when I was a good bit younger than you. That was in the days when this was a country. Come again. Any time. All you have to do is get on that thing and give us a ring. Fix you up with a bed at short enough notice. What do you say, Mally?'

'Yes. Of course, Daddy.'

'There you go then. That's all fixed. Probably see you again when you come to pick up your car in a day or so. Don't forget to let us know.'

'I won't,' said the Picaroon, and they took their leave shortly afterwards.

They had a quick run through to London, halting once on the way to assist a lady driver to change a tyre a few miles east of Reading.

She was a slight, grey-haired, spinsterish woman, and most grateful for their assistance. She was, she admitted, not very good at changing tyres. You needed strength for that sort of job.

The Picaroon agreed.

She was a nervous driver, she told them, and she had been in a bad crash. She had never really enjoyed driving since then, but, of course, one had to drive nowadays to get any place.

The Picaroon agreed with that too. There was visible evidence of the crash and he had been observant enough to notice it. The job finished, she had thanked them profusely, and the Picaroon and MacNab had got into their own car and had driven away, the Picaroon pondering a return in the near future to these pleasant parts.

In the event, he did not return to Hillmeet to pick up the car, for closer inspection revealed unsuspected damage and the Jaguar had to be transported to London. The days passed, became weeks and then months, and the Picaroon, a busy man, found that the exigencies of his calling deprived him of the time necessary for convivial jaunts. There was a four-month stint in Australia, followed by three months in the States. There was a quick trip to Montreal, from whence began a lengthy pursuit which led to British Columbia, California, Mexico, Guatemala and Barbados before Willi Ebbinhaus, a four-time killer, was laid to rest and the Picaroon, a little jaded from his wanderings, returned to the environs of S.W.5.

Oddly enough, he had once, in a Melbourne hotel come across an advertisement in an old copy of *The Times*, which had intrigued him considerably.

He had been reading an account of the big bullion robbery at the time, but the amazing fact that no less than three-quarters of a million pounds in gold bars had been hi-jacked on the road between Southampton and London, was of considerably less interest to him than the advertisement which ran :

FOR SALE : Quiet country house less than two hours by road from London. The Pines, Hillmeet, Berks. This desirable family residence consisting of : Ground Floor, Dining Room, Study, Morning Room, Cloak Room with wash basin and W.C. Kitchen Quarters etc. First Floor : Drawing-room, 4 Bedrooms, Two Bathrooms, Nursery —Usual Cupboards, Closets, etc. Top Floor : Three Attic Bedrooms, Bathroom. Two-car Garage. Toolshed. Coal-house. Greenhouse. Potting Shed. Large Garden with Small Cottage. This desirable Property is in excellent condition.
For particulars see : Maybury, Dyne and Stilton, 24A. Chadwick Lane, Lambourn.

The Picaroon had read it over twice and had looked at the date of the newspaper, which had been the third of May. The day on which he had read it was the eleventh of October. He produced a knife and slit out the advertisement carefully, placing it in his wallet for further reference.

Occasionally he found himself thinking of Mally Sheldon and of the bluff and cheerful commander, and wondering if in the end, the old man had decided he had indeed had a sufficiency of onions and had hied him to the sort of quiet coastal place he had once hinted at, there to mess about in a boat or two. But these sort of speculations were fruitless. Some day, he decided, he would be in England with a little time on his hands, and when that happy day arrived, he would take a little trip northwards and find out things for himself.

It was a comforting thought, but such nostalgic aspirations were never, in fact, to be achieved. And so the pages were removed from the calendar by time. Autumn gave way to the yellow fogs of winter, to frost and rime and long dark mornings became chill and cheerless dawns.

3

It was the week before Christmas. The air was cold and bleak and icy winds from the north-east hinted at snow, frost, sleet and such delights of the winter solstice as did the Picaroon's heart no good at all. He stood at the window of the sitting-room in the flat in Courtfield Mews and stared at the snowflakes which whitened the purple slates of an adjacent roof.

It was three o'clock. The fire burned cheerfully in the wide hearth and the magnolia-coloured walls were lit redly with fire-glow. There were Christmas cards on the mantelshelf and on each surface which could support them. There were cheerful little sprigs of holly, of mistletoe and ivy tucked into every corner where they might be accommodated, and from the kitchen premises came the deep and not unmusical basso-profundo of MacNab, polishing silver and keeping time, as he did so, to a plaintive Highland air.

The Picaroon sighed. 'What I don't understand, Mac,' he said, 'is why, with so many cheery songs to sing, you always have to cut loose with one of these tartan dirges.'

MacNab appeared in the doorway, a green baize apron round his ample waist, a spoon and a polishing cloth in his large hand. 'You don't like my singing?'

'I like the singing, but not the song.' The Picaroon shook his head. 'Think of it, Mac. Another day or two till Christmas. Presents, Christmas boxes, your hand never out of your pocket and with the Income Tax to follow on as soon as the New Year appears. Something with a bit more life in it would hit the spot a lot better.'

MacNab considered. 'I wouldn't say but what you're maybe right,' he said agreeably. 'The song I was singing is about a fisherman's daughter that gets turned into a seal and spends the time perusing about the sea shore watching her loved one cutting bracken on the hillside. It's a very tender thing, as you say yourself, but I wouldn't say it was maybe the cheeriest song you could have. What you want is the pipes. For general hilarity, there isn't anything like them.'

The Picaroon shuddered. 'Not for me, Mac. I prefer something milder.'

'A fiddle maybe.' MacNab was scornful. 'Not for me. Nothing to them but a squeak. There's no body. No weight. I wouldn't—'

The doorbell rang.

The Picaroon looked up with interest, 'We've got callers, Mac. I wonder who?'

MacNab removed his apron and laid it across the back of a chair. 'There's nothing like finding out. It can't be Wheat, because he doesn't know we've got back. It can't be the man who reads the meter, because Cole says he was here a week ago. It's a mystery and the best thing to do is to find out.' He stalked through to the front door, and the Picaroon heard it open.

There was the sound of voices. The door closed and footsteps approached.

MacNab led in a tall fair girl, beaming, 'You'll never guess!'

The Picaroon was startled. 'Mally! Mally Sheldon! Who'd ever have thought it!' He held out his brown, sinewy hand. 'How did you know we were back?'

The girl shook her head. 'I didn't even know you were away.'

Ludovic was annoyed. 'For more than a year now. Here and there. Everywhere. Canada, America, Australia, Singapore, Barbados. All these sort of places. Living out of suitcases, suffering privations of every sort and the girl didn't even know we'd been away. My dear child, we just got back. Ten days ago. That's so, Mac, isn't it?'

'Exact,' MacNab said.

'I shall not,' Ludovic began, 'describe these privations in detail. I have no wish to harry you, but we have suffered. I am right in saying so, Mac?'

'Ran out of whisky in South America.' MacNab shuddered in a fury of recollection. 'You couldn't think of a worse place to run out of spirits.'

'So there you are, Miss Sheldon.'

Mally said quietly, 'I'm not Miss Sheldon any more, Ludovic.'

'You're married?' The Picaroon was beaming. 'Sit down and tell me all about it, Mally. When did it all take place? Who is the lucky man? What does—?'

'Take your coat off first,' MacNab suggested. 'You'll get the benefit of it when you go out again.' He helped her off with it and drew up a chair by the fire. 'Just you sit down there, miss, and I'll get you something to put a heat in you.'

She sat down.

The Picaroon drew up a chair opposite her. 'This calls

for something out of the ordinary, Mally. We've got a bottle of champagne which is just waiting to—'

She said, 'No. I don't think so, Ludovic.'

'No champagne?'

'No.' She raised her eyes a little and he saw the desperation that flickered in them. 'I'm not in a mood for celebrating.'

'Something's gone wrong?'

'Yes—and very far wrong too.' She halted for a moment. 'That's why I'm here.'

'What do you mean?'

'It's Larry—my husband. He's disappeared.' Her mouth was quivering. She put a hand up to her lips and sat there pressing them.

MacNab rose briskly and made his way towards the kitchen.

The Picaroon leaned towards her. 'Disappeared?'

'Yes. I—I just can't understand it, Ludovic. Ten days ago. We've got a flat at Hampstead—in Eldridge Walk— 29, Eldridge Walk. We've been there ever since we got married. That was a year ago and—' She put her hands over her eyes, and kept them there. 'I've been out of my mind with worry about him, Ludovic. I've got no one to turn to. I couldn't think what to do, and then today I thought about you and I came here.'

'You couldn't have done a better thing,' the Picaroon said firmly.

MacNab came in with a trolley. On it was a pot of tea, a plate of mixed biscuits and a piece of cut cake. 'Here we are,' he said briskly. 'I've just made you a cup of tea and there's a biscuit or two to go along with it.'

The girl looked up. 'That is very sweet of you, Mr. MacNab.'

'Not a bit of it,' MacNab said. 'Just you drink it up. I've always noticed myself that when a lady is out of

21

sorts, there's nothing cheers her up again like a cup of tea. Just you get started and take your usual.'

She poured out a cupful, filled up a cup for the Picaroon. 'What about you, Mr. MacNab?'

'Not for me,' MacNab said frankly. 'I prefer whisky. I'll just take a spot just now to be sociable.' He produced a glass and did so.

Ludovic saw the hint of strain in her eyes, in the tight little lines at her mouth: then, 'You've sold your house at Hillmeet?'

She looked over at him. 'Yes. How did you know?'

'I saw the advertisement in *The Times*. I was in Australia at the time.'

'Daddy died.'

'I'm sorry to hear that,' Ludovic said quietly.

'His heart. It had troubled him for some time.' She thought for a moment. 'I sold the house and came up to London. That was when I met Larry Huth.'

Ludovic waited.

'Larry was with *Standard Press* at the time. He's a reporter. Just after we got married, he went to the *Post Courier*. That's where he is just now—only—only—' Tears were forming in her eyes. She raised a hand towards them.

'More tea,' MacNab said firmly. He poured it out for her.

'Thank you.' She began to stir it slowly. 'And now Larry's gone.'

'Ten days ago, you said?'

'Yes.' He was watching her fingers and they were tightly clenched. 'Ten days ago. He just disappeared without warning, without any word to me at all.' She looked at Ludovic with glassy eyes. 'I've been almost out of my mind with worry. His newspaper doesn't know where he is. I've gone to the police and they haven't been able to help. He's just gone. He's dropped out of life and—'

The Picaroon leaned over and placed one big, bronzed hand over her small white one. 'All right. Drink up your tea. After that—tell me about it.' He looked at her, smiling very reassuringly and sat back to listen.

4

'This is the nineteenth, isn't it? Well, it was ten days ago.' She held her chin up a little higher. 'I've hardly slept since then, Ludovic, with worry.' She thought for a moment. 'It was on Friday morning that I saw him last. We left the flat together about half-past eight in the morning.'

'You're working too?'

'Yes, with Miles and Frensham in Wickham Road.'

'What's their line?'

'Wine shippers. They're an old-established firm. I attend to their foreign correspondence.'

The Picaroon was impressed. 'It sounds pretty brainy, old girl.'

'Not really. I've got a flair for languages, that's all. Daddy was like that, though you **might** not have imagined it. He could speak fluent French, German, Italian, Russian and he was fairly proficient in Greek and Turkish and Arabic. It was just a flair he had. He passed it on to me. A great deal of it is aural, you know. His mother was an operatic singer and she passed her true ear to him and I inherited it. I've never had any trouble with languages, though I'm not nearly so good at correspondence. Anyway, that's what I do now.'

'So ten days ago you left home together at half-past eight in the morning.'

'Yes. We always travelled in by tube. If Larry was going to Fleet Street he carried on to Charing Cross and then to Blackfriars. I always left the tube first at Goodge Street and that's what I did that morning.'

'What happened then?'

'He just disappeared. I haven't seen him or heard from him since. Usually he rang me up at the office at least once a day. Mostly it was in the late afternoon when he was able to tell me when he'd be back to the flat. That day he didn't ring and even then I had a funny feeling about it. I mean, it was so unusual, because he hardly ever missed a day.'

'What happened then?'

'I went home as usual and half expected he might be at the flat when I got back. He wasn't. When he hadn't appeared by eleven o'clock, I rang the *Post Courier* and spoke to a man called Daly. Mr. Daly was surprised to hear he hadn't come home but he said he had no idea where he might be. He hadn't seen him himself, but as he'd come on late, he thought Larry must have been chasing up a story or something like that, and have run into a snag of some sort. Anyway, he was very nice about it and told me he'd make some inquiries and ring me back later.

'Well, he did, about half an hour later, but he couldn't tell me anything. Larry had been at his desk in the morning for a while, but he'd gone out around eleven o'clock, so far as he knew, no one had any idea where he'd gone.'

Ludovic considered. 'Was he working on a story?'

'They said—no.'

'What did they say?'

'Next morning I went up to the *Post Courier* to see Mr. Grant, the editor. He was very nice to me indeed, but he had no idea where Larry might be. He hadn't been sent out on a story and he ought to have seen Mr. Grant in the afternoon for a few moments. There had been a note on his desk to remind him about it, but he just hadn't turned up for it. Mr. Grant hadn't thought much about it at the time, but I could see he was puzzled. He said they'd put a girl on to checking the hospitals and they did that, but they got nothing out of it.'

'He didn't mention going to the police?'

'He did—but not until the following day when he rang up and told me they hadn't been able to find any trace of Larry. I wasn't too keen about doing that at first but I could see it was the sensible thing to do and so I agreed. Mr. Grant fixed up a meeting with an officer at Scotland Yard—an Inspector Banner.'

'And you saw him?'

'Yes. He was a very business like sort of person, but very pleasant. He took all the particulars and said he'd do what he could—but so far he hadn't had any word of him at all.' She looked up at Ludovic. 'He said they'd do what they could, but it wasn't the sort of case they could make much progress with. He said it was happening all the time. People disappearing from home and their work and that sort of thing, and that there was really very little the police could do about it because more often than not they wanted to disappear.'

There was a little break in her voice. 'Men trying to get away from their wives and families and responsibilities. In time, he said, they usually came back again and things were smoothed over. I told him it wasn't like that with Larry and me. That there wasn't any other woman involved, or debt or anything of that sort. I don't know that I convinced him, but I didn't need to. I was convinced myself.'

'Then there was nothing doing with the police?'

'No, I was pretty sure that for all I'd said, Inspector Banner wasn't going to be able to find Larry for me.'

She looked up. 'That was when I went to Jack Lockwood.'

The Picaroon looked interested. 'Who's Jack Lockwood?'

'He was on Daddy's ship.'

'Friend of the family?'

'Daddy thought a lot of him. He was master-at-arms. When he came out of the Navy, he went into partnership with his brother-in-law, Harry Tallman. Mr. Tallman had been a policeman in London and when he left the police force he had started a private inquiry agency. Jack Lockwood joined him there, but he didn't have very good luck, because quite shortly afterwards, Mr. Tallman was knocked down and killed by a bus, and Jack Lockwood has been trying to run the agency on his own since then.'

'But he isn't able to help?'

'Not so far. He said it was really a job for the police, but that the police were so much under strength just now that they would be very unlikely to do anything unless I could convince them that Larry was in some sort of danger, or that he had been threatened, or something of that nature, and of course, I couldn't do that.'

'So what happened?'

'Jack said he'd do what he could. By good luck he didn't have any other work in hand, so he said he'd look into it. That was last Wednesday.'

'And have you heard from him since?'

'Yes. I rang him up at his office on Thursday and he hadn't come in. He called me at the flat at night and said he'd been looking around, but he hadn't found out anything at all. He'd seen Inspector Banner and one or two people at the *Post Courier*, but he didn't sound very hopeful about it, and then on Saturday morning he rang me up at the flat again and this time I really thought he might have heard something.'

'He hinted at it, did he?'

She frowned. 'Not exactly. No, he didn't hint, but he seemed purposeful, if you know what I mean, as if he had an idea of some sort, although he didn't say he had. That was what I felt when I was speaking to him and I asked him, but he didn't give me an answer. All he did was ask me if I'd ever heard Larry mention someone called Harry Becker, but of course I hadn't and Lockwood just said he'd get in touch when he had something to report.'

Ludovic looked thoughtful. 'Harry Becker? And it means nothing to you?'

'Nothing at all. Larry didn't talk much about his work. When we were together at home, he liked to feel he was away from that sort of thing.'

'Wise man,' Ludovic said. 'And you haven't heard from Lockwood since?'

'Yes, I have,' she said quietly.

'When was that?'

'This morning I had a letter from him, advising me to call the whole thing off.'

'He did?' The Picaroon was staring.

'Yes. It was quite a nice letter.'

'Funny he didn't ring you.'

She smiled faintly. 'Well, I did think so myself and then I thought that he wouldn't feel very comfortable about turning me down and if he'd rung me up, I'd certainly have asked questions and it would have been embarrassing for him. Anyway, he sent me the letter, formally giving up the case. He was decent enough not to make a charge for the work he had done, but, of course, I shall pay him for that. I'm quite well off and I shouldn't want him to—'

The Picaroon said, 'Have you got the letter, Mally?'

She handed over a plain, white commercial-size envelope. It was addressed to her at Hampstead and had been franked at 4.30 at Earls Court post office.

The Picaroon drew out the single sheet of plain, white paper.

The letter had been typewritten, and it was easy to suppose that Jack Lockwood had done his own typing, and that it was not a skill he had learned in the Navy. It ran:

> 29 Gower Lane
> 18 December

Dear Miss Sheldon,

I am sorry to say that I have not been able to find any trace of your husband's movements since he disappeared. I have interviewed seven separate sources and have come to the conclusion that your best plan is to leave the matter to the civil police who are better equipped for dealing with missing persons.

I have decided to withdraw from the case as I do not wish to have to charge you fairly high rates for a job I am not able to carry out. I have also decided not to make a charge for the time I have put in so far, since I have not been able to help you.

I am sorry that I cannot continue, but it would only be money down the drain for you. I shall be very interested to hear from you after Mr. Huth has come back as I am sure he will.

> *Yours faithfully,*
> *Jack Lockwood*

The Picaroon read it over twice and passed it across to MacNab. 'Fair enough. I can see his point. At the same time—'

'I know, Ludovic. I can understand how he feels. Anyway, I just didn't know what to do after I read it. I rang him up, but he wasn't at his office. I went up at lunch time and he still wasn't there. And then I remembered you. Mr. Hudson, my boss, let me away a bit early so that I could come round here.'

MacNab returned the letter. 'He's no great hand at the typewriting, whatever he is. They used to say a sailor could do anything.'

The girl returned the letter to her handbag. 'That's all, Ludovic.' She looked at him earnestly. 'What do you think?'

He shook his head. 'It's too early to say anything about it. The police have investigated it. This editor chap, Grant, will have done the same. So has Lockwood and so far no one has made anything of it.'

She said quietly, 'Ludovic, I mentioned your name to Jack Lockwood.'

'How was that?'

'I said that if he couldn't help me I was going to see if you could.' She considered for a moment, then : 'Will you do something?'

Ludovic nodded. 'You don't need to ask. One or two questions now—and do your best to answer them. About Larry. Friends or relations who might know anything of his movements?'

'He's got no relatives in this country at all. He's an Australian. His father was German, but he'd been in Australia since 1924. Larry was born there. He was an only child and he knew nothing of any German relations. He wasn't at all interested in them, or in looking for them.'

'Friends, then?'

'He hasn't really got any close friends in England. He's only been here for two years and he busied himself pretty much in his work. He was very keen on it.'

'What sort of stories did he do?'

'Crime mostly.'

The Picaroon looked interested. 'Crime? That makes it interesting.'

'Not entirely. He covered other stories too. Some

municipal matters. Local government meetings and debates.'

'Schools and sewers?' Ludovic looked pensive. 'Not much in that, Mally. I like the crime angle best.' He thought for a moment. 'I want you to tell me what sort of fellow Larry is. I don't want a eulogy. I want to know what he's like. Give me a picture—and make sure the warts are left in.' He smiled at her.

The girl pondered. 'He's just very average, I suppose. Twenty-eight years old. He was brought up in Australia. He didn't go to university. Instead, he went straight into newspaper work on the *Adelaide Star* when he left school. He came to England two years ago just now and was with *Standard Press* for a year before he joined the staff of the *Post Courier*. He's about five feet eight, slim, fair with grey eyes and he's rather quiet. He's got a wonderful sense of humour and he's terribly kind. He's also very keen on his job.'

'But he doesn't talk about it to you.'

'No, he doesn't. We made that agreement when we got married at first, and it was his idea. No shop whatever, when we were at home. It was sensible too. After all, he had very long hours and very awkward ones and he felt if he came in late from his work, he would want to get away from it, not to sit around talking about difficulties and things that had happened during the day.'

'Wise man,' Ludovic said.

'It's a fact,' MacNab agreed solemnly. 'It's bad enough to have to do the work in the first place without having to talk about it when you might be enjoying yourself with a friendly dram in your hand.'

Ludovic said, 'You said he's keen on his job?'

'Very much so,' Mally told him, 'and he's good at it too. I'm sure he is.'

'What about his friends on the paper?'

'He doesn't talk about them very much.' She hesitated. 'He doesn't go into pubs if he can help it. He had a bad

30

duodenal ulcer before he left Australia and he can't drink at all, so he keeps away from temptation and that means he cuts himself away from a lot of fun with other reporters.'

'I can see that,' MacNab said compassionately.

The Picaroon produced a pad and pen. 'I want you to write down your home address, your office address and Lockwood's address. That should do to go on with.'

She wrote them down then laid the ballpoint pen on top of the pad and rose. 'I'll have to go now, Ludovic. I must get back to the office. It was very decent of them to let me get away for so long.'

MacNab helped her on with her coat. 'Just you get back to your work and don't bother your head. We'll see what has to be done about it.'

'That's right,' Ludovic said. He was looking at the list of addresses. 'I see you've put down your number. Good girl. I'll keep in touch. Don't expect too much for a day or two. These things take time and you can't rush them. Go home tonight. Take a couple of aspirins and a glass of hot milk before you go to bed, and you'll sleep like a child.'

'Tuts,' said MacNab, 'the very worst thing you could do. Aspirins! Not a worse thing you could put in your stomach. I was reading, myself there, not so long ago where a professor no less, was saying they cause bleeding in the stomach. Nobody wants the like of that. Take you a drop of the mountain dew and put it in an old cup in a pan of boiling water and heat it up till it's nice and hot. Stir in as much sugar as you need. There's some, like myself, that doesn't care for sugar. That's what to take going to your bed.'

The girl smiled. 'I'll think about it, Mr. MacNab. And now,' she was moving forwards when Ludovic said, 'One thing more, Mally. You said Larry was quiet. Was he always quiet?'

'Yes, I'd say so.'

31

'Then he was a droll-like Australian if he was,' MacNab said. 'The Australians I've met in with were all fine, cheery chaps as jovial as you like.'

'What was he like before this happened? Immediately before it happened? Was he quieter than usual, or was he just the same? Was he even a little excited or elated? In other words did you notice the slightest difference in his manner?'

She looked at him, frowning. 'You know, it's funny that you should say that, Ludovic.'

'You mean there was a change in his attitude?'

'I'm not really certain about it. I didn't notice it at the time, but, afterwards, looking back on it I think that on the Wednesday and Thursday he was excited about something. Not obviously so. He didn't show his feelings easily, Ludovic, but I've got the idea now that he was agitated in some way. Excited.'

'Alarmed or frightened?'

'It's hard to say,' she told him thoughtfully. 'More elated I'd say.'

'That's something,' the Picaroon said thoughtfully.

'Why do you ask?'

'I just want to know. I'll probably have to learn more about him yet.' He smiled down at her. 'That's that. We'll see what we can do, Mally. Just give me a day or two.' He took her arm and together they made their way to the front door.

5

MacNab was filling his pipe when the Picaroon came back a few moments later. The big man struck a match. 'If you ask me, it's going to be a bit of a caper.'

'That's true.' Ludovic dropped into a chair. 'When the police can't handle it, it isn't easy to see what we can do.'

'He could have walked out on her,' MacNab said bluntly. 'It's the first thing you think of, but I hadn't the heart to ask her.'

'I did,' Ludovic said. 'At the door.'

MacNab stared. 'Man, you must have a heart like a rate-collector. It's not me that could put it to her like that, I'll assure you. What did she say?'

'She's quite certain he didn't walk out on her. If he did, he walked out on his job at the same time. But she's quite positive there isn't another woman in whom he's interested, and I believe her, Mac. After all, they've only been married for a year.' He lit a cigarette, put his head back and let the smoke drift upwards. 'We haven't got very much, but what we have to do is make the best of what we have got.'

'You never said a truer word,' MacNab agreed devoutly. 'What have we got?'

Ludovic snapped his fingers. 'The police, this chap Grant, and Lockwood. We can have a word with them right away. That's going to clear the decks.' He looked at his watch. 'I'll check with Grant and I'll look up Lockwood. You might have a word with this Inspector Banner. I don't expect you'll get much there, but we can't afford to leave him out.' He rose as he spoke. 'Get that much tidied up and we can start fresh tomorrow.' He made his way through to the bedroom, dressed in a suit of his favourite grey, with a matching shirt and a maroon tie. When he came back, MacNab was on the telephone.

'Just so,' he was saying. 'I'll be along directly and we'll talk about it.' He hung up and looked across at Ludovic. 'That was Colin MacIver from Islay.'

'A friend of yours, Mac?'

'One of the best,' MacNab admitted. 'There never was a cheerier chap in this world, at five o'clock in the morning, with a bottle of Islay Mist in his stomach and it's me that should know, because many a night I've had with him. Sings like a lintie, if you give him half a chance, and the stories he can tell is fair beyond redemption.'

The Picaroon was mildly puzzled. 'An engaging character, Mac. But what's the idea in calling him just now?'

'He's at Scotland Yard,' MacNab said. 'It's the only thing anyone could have against his character. The last time I was with him he was talking about this Inspector Banner. I just thought I'd have a word or two with Colin before I went along. The thing is all right. Banner's on the job today, so I'll see him.' He moved through to the cloak-room and emerged in a voluminous tweed topcoat. 'That's that, are you ready?'

'I am. We'll take the tube,' Ludovic said and they made their way briskly to the underground station at Earls Court. 'One point, Mac. Don't mention Becker yet.'

'Trust me,' MacNab said.

It was five o'clock when the Picaroon left Blackfriars and went round to the large and ornate *Post Courier* building, and at the reception desk, the highly ornamental young lady to whom he spoke, was mildly doubtful.

'Mr. Grant is still in his office,' she admitted, 'but I'll be surprised if he does see you. He never sees anyone without an appointment and he hardly ever makes an appointment.'

'Try him,' the Picaroon advised. 'The name is Ludovic

34

Saxon.' He watched her make a note of it. 'Suggest to him that the purpose of my visit to him is to discuss Larry Huth.'

She looked up quickly. 'Our Larry Huth?'

'That's the fellow. Know him?'

'Yes, indeed. He's very nice.' She lifted the receiver and spoke into it. When she laid it down she looked at him a little curiously. 'You're to go up, Mr. Saxon.' She beckoned to a messenger. 'Mr Saxon to see Mr. Grant, Collins.'

'This way, sir,' said Collins and the Picaroon tip-toed reverently after him.

Grant's office was on the second floor. Grant was behind his desk, a tall, sandy East Coast Scot with a long, half-humorous face and grey, steady eyes. He rose when the Picaroon came into the room, and came round the desk to shake hands. 'Mr. Saxon, I don't think we've ever met, but we've told the world about you from time to time.' He pointed to a chair. 'Sit down.' He went back to his own chair, lifted a pipe from the desk and began to fill it. 'Smoke if you want to. I can offer you a fill.'

'Thank you,' said Ludovic. He lit a cigarette.

Grant struck a match and when his pipe was drawing satisfactorily, 'You came up to talk about Larry Huth?'

'I came up to hear about him,' Ludovic told him.

'A friend of yours?'

Ludovic shook his head. 'I'd never heard of him until this afternoon. But his wife is a friend of mine. I had a visit from her today. She is very distressed and she asked me to help. I'll do what I can. That's why I'm here, Mr. Grant.'

Grant nodded. 'I see. Well, I'll give you what I've got, but I have to warn you now it's not going to amount to any more than Mrs. Huth was able to tell you.' He took the pipe out of his mouth. 'Frankly, all I can say is that I've got no idea what happened to Huth. He walked out of his office ten days ago—round about eleven o'clock in the morning. He spoke to one of the girls on the desk. He spoke to the cashier and left the building. So far as I know, no one has come forward to say he's been seen since.'

'Who was the girl at the desk?'

'Anne Pennant. You won't get anything there. All he said to her was "I saw your boy friend last night, Anne." I've questioned her about it. So have the police. It didn't get us anywhere, because she hasn't got a boy friend.'

Ludovic looked interested. 'Not interested in boys?'

Grant laughed. 'I'm afraid I didn't express myself very well, Mr. Saxon. What I should have said is that she's got stacks of them. She's a very attractive girl—but there's no particular boy friend. She didn't ask him who he meant. If she'd done that it might have helped. She only laughed and Huth went along and drew five pounds from the cashier and left.'

'What did he say to the cashier?'

'Nothing that would help. Keech thought he was in a rather thoughtful mood. All he did was fill out a voucher and say that it was a cold day.'

'It isn't much help.'

'It isn't,' Grant agreed. 'You can see Miss Pennant if you wish. Keech, no. He's down with 'flu.'

Ludovic sighed. 'It hardly seems necessary, Mr. Grant. I'm hoping I'll get enough from you to get started. You don't mind if I ask you some questions about Huth?'

'Go ahead.'

'What sort of a fellow is he? I've had his wife's opinion. I'd like another point of view.'

A smile flickered in the grey eyes. 'I liked him. He was a very decent little fellow, and he was a damned good reporter.' He leaned forward. 'He was keen, ambitious and he had a nose for a story. More than that, he'd take the trouble to run facts into the ground. He didn't spare himself on the job. I had a lot of faith in him. He was the sort of fellow who'd make a name for himself.'

'He was that good, was he?'

'Give him five years and he'd be at the top,' Grant said crisply. 'I know what I'm talking about, Mr. Saxon. I've been forty-three years in Fleet Street, and all the really first class men I've met, I could count on the fingers of these two hands.' He held them up. 'Huth, with five years' experience, would be one of them. Does that satisfy you?'

The Picaroon nodded. 'So far as his work is concerned, yes.'

'And that's all I'm qualified to talk about,' Grant said.

He frowned as he spoke. You're not going to find it easy to get first-hand information about him. He isn't one of your cheery, slap-you-on-the-back-and-have-one type. To begin with, he doesn't drink, because he's got an ulcer which plays him up if he does. You won't find him in pubs very often. At the Press Club for a meal occasionally. That's about all. He's not particularly good in company. You could be with him for a night without noticing him at all, but he is outstandingly good at his job. He's got ability, drive, ambition, all of which I've already mentioned. He's got something else I haven't mentioned. Integrity.'

Ludovic looked over at him. 'That's interesting.'

'It is,' Grant said. 'There's not too much of it going around these days.' He took the pipe out of his mouth again. 'You haven't asked me the inevitable question. Has he gone away with another woman? My answer, without waiting for the question is—no! He's not the sort. He's in love with his wife and that's that!'

'Was he working on any special sort of job?'

Grant shook his head. 'No, I've looked into that most carefully. Just routine stuff for the past few weeks. You don't get big stories breaking right, left and centre and the routine jobs have to be done. He's done one or two feature articles recently. One was on the value of space flights. Another was on professional football. He attended one or two meetings of the Greater London Council. He's looked in at Westminster. Now he's gone.' He smiled at Ludovic as he spoke. 'That's all I can tell you. But the police are a bit worried, I imagine. They're afraid we'll come out with a blast. We won't. Not yet.' He looked at the clock. 'And now, Mr. Saxon, I'm afraid I can't spare you any more time.' He reached towards the box as he spoke. 'Would you like to speak to Miss Pennant?'

The Picaroon thought it might be a good idea.

Grant flicked a switch. 'Mr Saxon is leaving now. He wants to have a word with Miss Pennant. Tell her she's to give him all the assistance she can.' He rose and as he did so, the door opened and a commissionaire appeared.

Grant held out his hand. 'Good luck, Mr. Saxon. I'll be interested to hear what you make of it.' He sat down again.

Ludovic went out and downstairs to the reception desk where a dark, attractive girl was waiting for him.

She smiled at him as he came towards her. 'Mr. Saxon?'

'In person.'

'I'm Anne Pennant. Mr. Grant says you want to speak to me.' She indicated a doorway in one corner. 'Shall we go in there?'

'It seems a good idea,' Ludovic agreed and followed her into a small room furnished with four deep armchairs, a table and a selection of ashtrays.

She sat down. 'It's about Mr. Huth, isn't it?'

He nodded. 'He spoke to you before he left the building?'

'Yes, he did.' She looked at him curiously. 'He didn't really say very much though, but Mr. Grant and the police have asked me about it.'

'What happened?'

'Well, my desk is next to the cashier's cage as you probably noticed. Mr. Huth was waiting to get some

38

money, but someone was already talking to Mr. Keech, the cashier, so Mr. Huth had to wait. I was standing beside him and he looked round at me and said, "Hullo, Anne." Then he smiled and said, "I saw your boy friend last night." That was all he said.'

'And what did you say?'

'I didn't have a chance to say anything because Kitty Anstey, who was getting money from Mr. Keech, moved away and Mr. Huth moved along to take her place. That was all that was said.'

'And whom did he mean?'

'That's what Mr. Grant wants to know, but I can't say. Mr. Huth didn't mention a name.' She frowned a little. 'Anyway, I was a bit surprised, because Mr. Huth had never spoken to me like that before. He's always very reserved.'

Ludovic looked at her pensively. 'Didn't make little jokes with the girls?'

'No, he didn't. It wasn't that he was stuffy or anything like that, just that he was shy. Anyway, he didn't have much to do with any of the girls I know about. We often wondered why, and then we heard he was getting married and—' She made a gesture. 'Well, that sort of explained it.'

'I suppose so. So you don't know whom he did mean?'

'No. I was curious,' she admitted. 'I've got half-a-dozen boy friends. Ted Armitage. Matt Smedley. Rickie Steedman—oh, a whole dozen.'

'Any of them work here?'

'No—none of them. That's what puzzled me. Even if he had met someone, how was he to know he was a friend of mine?'

'That is the question,' the Picaroon said.

'I've been racking my brain to puzzle it out ever since.'

'Keep on trying,' Ludovic said. 'That's all you can remember?'

'It's all that happened,' she said. 'Now I'll have to get back to the desk.'

Ludovic opened the door for her. 'Funny that should be the last thing he should say before he went adrift. It had to mean something.'

'That's what Mr. Grant thought, but it doesn't mean anything to me.' She looked round at him. 'Do you know what, Mr. Saxon? I don't think he meant anything at all. I think he was just joking, even if it was out of character.'

'I don't,' said the Picaroon thoughtfully. He followed her into the wide, marble foyer. 'Thank you, Miss Pennant. Keep thinking about it. One of these days you'll probably guess what he meant. If you do, give me a ring at this number.' He gave her a little white card. 'Good-day to you.'

A minute later, he was in the street, heading for Gower Lane.

6

Gower Lane was grey, narrow and twisted. The Picaroon turned in at the entrance to 29 and made his way up a dark, well-worn stairway to the third floor, on which level the firm of Tallman and Lockwood had their office and found this was at the far end of a dark and narrow corridor. He halted at the door and stood listening for a moment, but there was no sound from within. Across the door itself the designation TALLMAN & LOCK-WOOD had been stencilled in black, but a not very satisfactory attempt had been made to paint out Tall-man's name.

The Picaroon tried the handle of the door and found it locked. For a moment or so he stood there considering, then made his way back along the corridor to the first door on his left, and from the room beyond, he heard the steady clatter of a typewriter. Stencilled on the door itself was the inspiriting designation :

KLEIN & WEISSMAN

Importers & Agents

RING AND ENTER

The Picaroon rang and entered. He found himself in a small and not uncomfortable office. A fire burned cheer-fully in an old-fashioned fireplace, and in front of this a pale, fair-haired girl sat at a desk, typing.

She looked up in some surprise as Ludovic appeared and Ludovic noticed that as well as being a pale, fair girl, she was a bad case of acne. She stopped typing and said, 'Afternoon, sir. If it's Mr. Klein, you're out of luck. He's in Manchester all week. Next week it's Liverpool.'

'Gracious me!' said the Picaroon. 'He sees life, doesn't he?'

'Mr. Klein? He gets around, sir. Since Mr. Weissman died he runs the business himself. I do the work here at the office—all of it. Not that there's such a lot to do, but the hours are long. Keeps me here a lot, if you know what I mean?'

The Picaroon did know what she meant and decided that this was the moment for a surprising revelation. 'In fact it wasn't Mr. Klein I wanted to see, it was your next door neighbour—Mr. Lockwood.'

'Oh!' She looked interested. 'Mr. Lockwood isn't at the office today.'

'He certainly isn't in just now.'

41

'Nor yesterday either,' she said. 'He nips in here quite a lot when he's at the office to speak to me. He's a very nice man.'

'Friend of yours?'

She laughed. 'Well, you know how it is. I'm alone here most of the time. Not many people call to see Mr. Klein. I'm always glad to see Mr. Lockwood. There's always a cup of tea going here at eleven o'clock and Mr. Lockwood usually pops in with a couple of cakes from Lieber's cake shop at the corner.'

'And quite right too,' the Picaroon said. 'You said Lockwood wasn't in his office yesterday either. You're sure of that?'

She was quite certain. Lockwood always looked in as soon as he arrived. Usually he did so before he went to his own office at all.

'I'm in at a quarter-to-nine,' she explained, 'but quite often it's eleven or so before he arrives. He keeps funny hours. He usually asks me if I've heard his 'phone ringing.'

The Picaroon nodded. 'He hasnt' got a girl in the office then?'

'No. There's not enough need for one. I sometimes get people coming in here looking for him just as you're doing, and I usually take their names and addresses. If you want to give me yours, I'll tell him you've called.'

The Picaroon looked thoughtful. 'A girl would be handy for him, you know. She could do his office work and typing for him.'

She shook her head. 'There isn't enough work to keep a girl busy—and, anyway, I do his typing for him and it doesn't amount to much. Mostly it's accounts or an odd letter. He hasn't got a typewriter of his own. I run odd things off for him here and he gives me something for it. Now if you'd like to give me your name and—'

'I think I'll call on him,' Ludovic said. 'You don't

happen to have his home address, do you?'

She nodded. 'I can find it for you.' She opened a drawer and produced an address book. 'Here it is. Care of Asher, 37 Pelling Lane, Earls Court.'

The Picaroon jotted it down. 'Good of you, old girl. I'll nip up and see him now on my way home.' He thanked her and took his leave, a thoughtful man, tried Lockwood's door again, then went down to the street.

He made his way by tube to Earls Court, and sought Pelling Lane.

It was a short, narrow street of tall houses, all of them long since converted into bed-sitters and 37 was a corner house with a door on two streets.

The Picaroon touched the bell, and waited. A moment or so passed, then he heard the sound of footsteps hurrying along a stone hallway.

The door opened. A tall, elderly woman looked out at him.

The Picaroon removed his hat. 'Good evening. Mrs. Asher?'

'Yes, I'm Mrs. Asher.'

'I've called to see Mr. Lockwood.'

She looked mildly startled. 'Mr. Lockwood? Yes—but he isn't in at present.'

'When will he be back?'

She had a rather long face with high cheek bones and now it was slightly flushed. 'I'm not sure about that.' She hesitated, 'Are you a friend of Mr. Lockwood's?'

'I'm a friend of a friend,' Ludovic told her. 'I've just come from his office in Gower Lane. He wasn't there. He hasn't been there for a couple of days now.' He stopped to look at her. 'I'm a little bit worried about it.'

'So am I,' she said. She held the door open a little more widely. 'Come in for a moment, Mr.—'

'Saxon.' He stepped into the hall.

She closed the door and pointed to another no more than six feet away. 'That's his room. He's been there with me for six years now. A very pleasant gentleman and no bother to get on with at all. I don't like it, Mr. Saxon—I haven't seen him since yesterday morning.'

'He was here then?'

'Yes. He went out earlier than usual. He got breakfast at eight o'clock and I heard him leave shortly before nine. Usually he doesn't go out till closer to nine-thirty or even ten oclock.'

'And he hasn't come back since?'

'No, indeed.' She stared at him. 'You know he's never done that before. Keeps late hours, mark you—but that's his job, and he has been out all night a few times too, but he always told me or rang up or something any other time. That's why I'm upset about him saying nothing this time. It's not like him.'

'He didn't leave a note in his room?'

'He wouldn't need to.' She thought for a moment, then produced a key and opened the door, then stepped inside.

The Picaroon followed her in.

The room was square, high-ceilinged and comfortably furnished. There was a divan bed against one wall, an electric fire, a wash basin, a bookcase with a number of books in it. There was a tall oak wardrobe, and on one wall a pipe-rack with three or four pipes in it.

She was looking about her. 'No note. Do you think I should phone the police?'

Ludovic pondered. 'It does seem a bit drastic. I'd give him another twenty-four hours. If he hasn't got in touch by that time, I think you should.'

She led the way out to the hall. 'All right, I shall. It worries me. You hear of such dreadful things happening these days. He could have been run over by a bus or something.' She opened the front door for him. 'I'll do as you say, Mr. Saxon. I'll wait till tomorrow. If he isn't here by tomorrow night at this time, I'll phone up the police and tell them about him.'

'Do that,' the Picaroon said and asked a question.

She shook her head. 'No, he hasn't got a typewriter here. At his office perhaps.'

He thanked her and took his leave.

A quarter of an hour later he was at the flat in Court-field Mews. MacNab had not yet returned, and he lit a cigarette and settled down in front of the fire to ponder the events of the afternoon.

Ten days ago, Larry Huth had disappeared. Now it looked very much as though Jack Lockwood had done likewise.

For half an hour by the clock, Ludovic Saxon sat staring into the fire considering the situation which had arisen and at the end of that time he sighed and lit a fresh cigarette. 'These things are sent to perplex us,' he said aloud, and as he did so he heard the sound of a key turn in the lock, the door open and close.

A moment later, MacNab came into the room.

7

The big man was smiling as he appeared. 'I see you're back. I was wondering about that. You'll be ready for a meal and I'm the boy that's looking forward to one myself. It'll be a good one, I'll assure you of that. A mixed grill. Everything's in order. Steak, kidneys, sausages, mushrooms, the lot. Just you wait till I put on the gas and peel an onion or two.' He disappeared and when his culinary preparations had been disposed of, he came through lighting his pipe.

Ludovic looked up at him. 'How did you get on with Banner?'

MacNab crossed towards the decanter. 'Just you wait the one wee minute till I get myself a refreshment. Cooking is dry work.' He brought his glass back to the fire and sat down with every appearance of relaxed enjoyment. 'Here's to your good health. Banner? I had a long talk with him. A fine young man. He'll go far that one if he keeps his health and strength.'

'Has he got anything?'

'He has not,' MacNab said with conviction. 'And it hasn't been for trying. He's spent more time on the job than he should because Grant is an important man and Grant was putting the pressure on him. For all that he hasn't got anything at all.'

'What does he think about it?'

'He's puzzled.'

'It doesn't take much to puzzle a policeman,' Ludovic said and MacNab gloomily admitted the truth of this suggestion.

'It's a fact. They're not what you might call as smart on the uptake as you or me. Nothing against their character, mind you. I've got four cousins yonder that's in the force and I know what I'm talking about. Fine, fine fellows when you get them out of uniform and a glass in their hands. As cheery as you like but when they're on duty you lose taste of them altogether. Different men.' He brooded for a moment.

'Banner thinks Huth must have disappeared deliberately. He can't think of any other reason than he's taken up with another woman, or that someone has threatened him and he's gone into hiding.'

Ludovic shook his head. 'Why didn't he let his wife know?'

MacNab looked thoughtful. 'There is many a thing that happens to a man he doesn't let his wife know about,' he said sagely. 'So they tell me. Them that's got wives. I never had one myself. I was always too busy with one thing and another. Anyway I asked Banner about that. He thinks there could be another woman. He's seen the young lady and he doesn't think it very likely, but he has to think something. What about you?'

'Grant can't explain Huth's disappearance.' He gave MacNab an account of his interview with the editor and the big man nodded.

'It doesn't help. What about Lockwood?'

The Picaroon considered him. 'Huth disappeared ten days ago. Now, as far as I can see, Lockwood has disappeared too. He hasn't been seen since yesterday morning.'

'Mighty me!' MacNab took a pull at his glass.

'I called at his office. He hasn't been there. I called at his boarding-house. His landlady's worried that he's been gone without a word since yesterday morning. It seems he's never done that before.' He looked at MacNab. 'There's something else.'

MacNab rose briskly. 'That's the potatoes boiling over. Just you wait till I see that everything's in order.' He left the room to return in a moment or two. 'I poured them while I was at it. You were saying there was something else.'

Ludovic nodded. 'That letter Mally showed us. It was typewritten.'

'It was that,' MacNab agreed. 'And none too well typewritten either.'

'I had a word with the girl in the office next door. Lockwood got her to do his typing for him. He didn't have much to do and he hasn't got one in his office.'

MacNab pondered. 'There's other places than his office where a man can keep a typewriter. He could have it at home.'

'I had a look around his room. It wasn't on display. His landlady says he hasn't got one there. She's quite sure of that. He's been with her for six years and she'd have seen it or heard it if he had.'

There was a little silence.

MacNab said thoughtfully, 'I know what you're thinking.'

'I'm thinking that Lockwood didn't send that letter to Mally Sheldon at all,' Ludovic said quietly.

'Then who sent it?'

The Picaroon beamed. 'That, Mac, is the jolly old question.'

'It's a puzzle.'

'And we're going to find the answer to it,' Ludovic said. 'Huth goes adrift and Mally puts this chap Lockwood on to him. Now Lockwood has gone A.W.O.L.'

'Watch it doesn't happen to you,' MacNab counselled.

'It might be a good thing if it did.'

MacNab rose briskly. 'Maybe it would and maybe it wouldn't. It's time I was getting on with the grill. The potatoes will be spoiling on me.' He went through to the kitchen and the Picaroon approached the telephone.

He put through a call and, when he heard the voice of the operator at the other end, 'Ludovic Saxon. May I speak to Mr. Saltmarsh?'

Peter Saltmarsh came on a moment later. 'Hullo, Ludovic. You've just got me as I was leaving. Got my coat on, in fact. I hope it's nothing important.'

'It could be,' Ludovic said, 'but not at this moment. I might need you to do some work on it later. All I want now is some information. Do you know an ex-navy type in your line of business called Lockwood?'

'Jack Lockwood? Tallman and Lockwood?'

'That's the chap.'

'I know him all right.' Peter Saltmarsh said. 'Lockwood's all right. In fact I've had him working for me once or twice when I was pushed and couldn't cover an odd job. What can you want to know about him?'

'As much as you can tell me.'

'All I can tell you about is that he's a sound, reliable man. I liked him and I'd have given him a permanent job, only he didn't want that. He runs a small agency. It used to belong to his brother-in-law who was in the Metropolitan Police at one time. Tallman had done a few chores for me. He's dead now but Lockwood carries on. Why are you asking about him?'

The Picaroon told him.

Peter Saltmarsh was mildly surprised. 'It isn't like Lockwood to back out of a job, I can tell you that. He's the bulldog breed. From what you say, it looks to me as though he's got on to something and someone has stepped on his fingers.'

'That's what I think,' Lockwood agreed. 'I saw the letter. It was typewritten with his signature at the end of it.' He thought for a moment. 'Right, Peter, I'll look into it. It isn't going to be easy, because so far as I know he ran a one man business. No help at all. My guess is that he wouldn't even trouble with case cards. Think about it. If you can put your finger on any angle, I'll be obliged. Goodnight.'

'I'll do that,' Saltmarsh said and hung up.

The Picaroon did likewise.

MacNab was wheeling in the trolley. He said, 'Here we are. The very best beef out of Wilson the butcher's, and, man, but it's an awful price. Sit you down and we'll get started.' He sat down himself, tucked a napkin into position and busied himself. 'What did Peter say?'

The Picaroon told him.

'A sound man,' MacNab said. 'He must be if he worked for Peter. All right, where is he now? That's the question.'

Ludovic dissected the steak. 'Take it that Lockwood got exactly the same as we did from the girl, Mac. If he did, he's got a whisper of something.'

MacNab looked up. 'You're thinking about Harry Becker?'

49

Ludovic nodded. 'Lockwood asked her if she'd ever heard Huth mention Becker. She says she never did.'

'If Huth was in Fleet Street for a year he would know Becker,' MacNab said.

'He would know a lot of people,' Ludovic agreed, 'but that's not to say he would be likely to mention all of them to his wife. In any event, you heard what she said. He had a thing about discussing his work when he was at home.'

'And he had the right idea,' MacNab said firmly. 'There's a time and place for everything, and a home is some place you can put your feet up and forget all those kind of worries.' He pushed his chair back. 'I'll get the biscuits and cheese. That's a fine, fine bit of Stilton there. The best that money can buy.' He came back in a moment or two with it on a tray. 'What are you going to do?'

'See Becker.'

MacNab thought it over. 'Do you think it's the wise thing to do? It looks to me as if maybe Huth had known Becker and went up to see him, and Lockwood did the same. What do you think yourself?'

'I think maybe you're right,' Ludovic said, and there was a dancing little light in his eyes. 'Huth called on Becker and went adrift. Lockwood called on Becker and went adrift. Now I'm going to call on Becker.'

'Watch that you don't do the same.'

The Picaroon poured out a coffee. 'You'll be on the job, Mac, to see that I don't.' He spooned sugar into his cup and for the next few moments spoke very precisely indeed.

8

Harry Becker was a strongly built man in his late forties, broad-shouldered and running a little bit to flesh nowadays. He had pleasant ruddy features, blue eyes and his own fair hair, thick and luxurious, was plentifully shot with grey. He dressed well, wore beautifully tailored suits and linen that was irreproachable. He sat in his well appointed office in Prior Lane behind a stout oak door on which was tastefully lettered,

BECKER & KNIGHTLY

Importers

and looked thoughtfully at the drab little man who sat on the opposite side of the desk.

'I don't know, Lappin,' he said. 'You'll have to give me time to think about it. Time to look around. It might be I could hear of someone. I'm not saying I would, mind you. You don't hear about these kind of people every day, but I'll do what I can. Come back in a week.'

'Very good, Mr. Becker, I'll be here. You can tell anybody that's interested this thing I got in mind is as safe as houses. There's money in it too.'

'We'll hope so,' Becker said good-naturedly. 'Right, Lappin. Goodnight to you.' He watched Lappin move towards the door.

It opened as he did so, and Spahn let the little man out. Spahn was tall, broad-shouldered and blue-chinned, an ex-boxer and a very useful man to have around. Harry Becker had had him around for a long time. Now he looked up at him.

'Anyone else, Lew?'

'Elke.' Spahn was a man of few words and those few were mostly unprintable.

Becker nodded. 'Send him in.'

Elke was ushered in a moment later. He was a thin, weary-looking man of fifty, bald as an egg and quite expressionless. He sat down on the chair opposite to Becker without invitation, for he was a frequent caller.

'Evening, Mr. Becker.'

'Evening, Bert.' Becker pushed a box of cigarettes across towards him.

Elke took one, struck a match against his nail and lit up. He sat for a moment then leaned forward. 'I'm on to something good, Mr. Becker.'

'What is it?'

'Pussy-cat job,' Elke explained. 'From what I've got it should be good.'

'How good?'

'Thirty thousand quid in furs.'

'Where is it?'

'Plantation Alley. Deacon's warehouse.'

Mr. Becker rubbed a plump hand across his lip. 'What do you need?'

'There has to be four of us,' Elke said. 'There's me an' Ted Spicer. I need two men. I know where I can get them if I can put enough sugar in the cup.'

'How much?'

'A monkey apiece.'

Becker nodded. 'Fair enough.' He thought for a moment. 'Tell you what, Bert, I'll put it around. Give me a little time and I'll maybe hear of someone.'

'Hearing of someone' was Harry's speciality. You wanted a job done, you came to him for what you needed. Men, money, a lorry—and he listened to you and if he liked the sound of what you told him, there was always the chance he would hear of someone who might be interested. He never knew of anyone. Knowing was too positive for Harry Becker, but he usually managed to hear of someone who would accommodate.

Elke leaned forward. 'It'll have to be sooner that that, Mr. Becker. The tip I've got is that the stuff could be moved up north within a week.'

Becker pondered. 'Come back tomorrow. Same time.'

Elke pushed aside his chair as he rose. 'I'll be here tomorrow, Mr. Becker.'

'Good,' said Harry. He touched the push of the buzzer on his desk. When Spahn came in he said, 'Bert is just leaving. Anyone else?'

'Just Bullitt.'

Becker shook his head. 'No. Chase him.'

Spahn followed Elke into the ante-room, closing the door behind him.

Harry Becker sat back, lit a cigarette and stroked his plump, round cheek. He lifted the receiver at his hand, dialled a number, and when he got through, 'Becker here.'

'Yes?' The voice at the other end was quiet and level.

'I've just had a chap here,' Mr. Becker said, 'with a whisper about something that sounds good.'

'How good?'

'A pussy job. There could be thirty thousand in it. That's his story.'

'Is he reliable?'

'Yes, it was Elke. He's sound enough. He needs two men and a lorry. He can get the men for a monkey a head.'

'He shouldn't have any difficulty.'

Becker said, 'He's pushed for time. He says the stuff is being moved north within a week.'

There was a little silence. 'Give him what he wants. You can manage the lorry?'

'Yes, I've heard of one that's available for a price.'

'What's the price?'

'Two ton.'

'Fix it.' There was a click as the line went dead.

Mr. Becker laid down his own receiver and reached for another cigarette. His hand was groping in the box when he was suddenly aware that the door had opened and closed and that the key had been gently turned. He looked up very quickly.

'Hello, Harry,' said the Picaroon.

Becker stared. His fleshy features were suddenly pale.

'Remember me?'

Mr. Becker nodded. 'Saxon, isn't it? Fellow they call the Picaroon.'

'That's right,' Ludovic agreed. He came across and sat down on the end of the desk, looked into the silver box and shook his head admiringly. 'Self-indulgent little character, Harry, aren't you? Nothing but the best for Mr. Becker.'

Harry Becker licked his lips. 'How did you get in?'

The Picaroon jerked his head backwards. 'That way.'

'There's a fellow out there to stop that kind of thing happening.'

'Lew Spahn,' Ludovic said. 'He's still there. I wouldn't say he's in the best of good health, mark you. You might need to get another one.' He produced a lighter, lifted a cigarette and struck a light. He put his head back and drew in smoke. 'Spahn never was much good. He hasn't improved with keeping.'

Harry Becker had recovered himself. Now he laughed. 'You will have your little joke, Mr. Saxon.'

'That's right. That's me all over.'

'What do you want here?'

Ludovic looked down at him. 'I've known about you for a long time, Becker. You're a nasty little man. I've got one or two things chalked up against you.'

Becker smiled feebly. He was listening for some sound or movement in the ante-room and hoping he heard it soon. Himself, he was a realist and he had no illusions at all as to what the Picaroon was capable of doing if he were in the mood for violent action. There was no

54

sound at all from the outer room and his uneasiness grew.

The Picaroon, as though he had been precisely aware of what was going on in his mind, said, 'Spahn's out. He'll be out for half an hour yet. There's a little vein in your neck, Becker, and if someone presses on it and—'

'Sure. Sure, Mr. Saxon.' Becker was not anxious to discuss veins in his neck. 'Let's forget Spahn, Mr. Saxon. You didn't come here to talk about Spahn. Something I can do for you, Mr. Saxon? If there is—all you have to do is name it. Glad to help out. If you've got a problem of some sort, Mr. Saxon, you leave it with me.'

'A problem there is,' Ludovic said.

Harry Becker sighed. 'We've all got them, Mr. Saxon. What is it?'

'Remember Jack Lockwood?'

A little light flickered in Becker's pale blue eyes.

'I can see you do,' said the Picaroon.

Becker frowned. 'Lockwood? Lockwood? Let me think, Mr. Saxon.'

'Think quickly,' said Ludovic. 'Jack Lockwood, a private investigator. He's got a business in Gower Lane.'

Becker shook his head. 'An investigator? I wouldn't know him.'

'You're sure of that?'

'Couldn't be surer,' Becker said. 'I've got a pretty good memory, Mr. Saxon. I meet a lot of people in my job. Naturally, you don't expect me to remember the names of them all, but I get most of them. Every now and then one gets by, but I can't think of this Lockwood. I say I've never met him.'

'He says he's met you though.'

Becker's face was suddenly wooden. 'Mistake, Mr. Saxon. We all make 'em. I know a few private operators, naturally.'

'Naturally,' Ludovic agreed.

'But not this one. Not a Lockwood. What's so special about this one?'

'This one,' said the Picaroon, 'has suddenly gone adrift, Becker. Very suddenly. Too suddenly in fact. I've called round to let you know he'd better come to the surface again very, very soon.' Ludovic pressed out the butt of his cigarette in the ashtray. 'If he doesn't, Becker, I'll be chasing you up. Understand?'

Becker's face was suddenly grey. He swallowed once or twice. 'Look here, Mr. Saxon, I don't know this character you talk about. I can't help you there.'

'Pity,' said the Picaroon. He walked to the door, fitted the key into the lock and turned it. He looked back bleakly. 'You've got till tomorrow to find out about him, Harry. You're a fixer. One of the best contact men in the business, so they tell me. Now's your chance to do yourself a little bit of good. Do a bit of real fixing while you're still around and able to attend to things. Good-night, Harry.' He closed the door and Harry Becker heard the sound of his feet as he crossed the floor of the ante-room.

The door opened and closed and the room was very very still.

9

For a long moment, Harry Becker sat still at his desk, then, cautiously, he rose and crossed to the door. He opened it fractionally and listened, but there was only the sound of heavy breathing from the far corner. He opened it a little more widely and peered over to where

Spahn lay draped across an armchair on the opposite side of the ante-room.

He closed the door cautiously, locked it and returned to his desk. Now he sat down behind it, drew the telephone towards him and began to dial a number. When he was through, a woman's voice said: 'Smail and Usher.'

'This is Mr. Becker. I'd like to speak to Mr. Usher.'

'Mr. Usher has a client just now.'

Harry Becker licked his lips. 'It's very urgent, Miss Prosser. Will you see if you can do anything?'

She hesitated for a moment. 'If you would care to give the message to me I could—'

'No, no. That wouldn't do at all. It's confidential. Highly confidential. Ask him to ring me when he gets through with his client.'

'If it really is as important as all that, Mr. Becker, I'll take him in a message. Hold the line for just a moment and I'll see.'

A moment or so passed. There was the sound of the receiver being lifted.

'Simon Usher speaking.'

'This is Becker, Mr. Usher. I've just had a visitor.'

'Who was that?'

'Saxon. This fellow they call the Picaroon.'

There was a little silence.

'He walked in on me,' Becker said incoherently. 'Knocked Spahn out or something and came through to me. I've just got rid of him.'

'What did he want?'

'He wanted information about Lockwood,' Becker said. 'Shook me a bit, Mr. Usher. I told him I'd never heard of him. I don't know whether he believed me or not. Anyway, I put him off. Till tomorrow, at any rate. He said he'll be back then.'

'Interesting,' said Mr. Usher. 'Until tomorrow. How do you propose to cope then?'

'I won't be here,' Becker said bluntly. 'I know this fellow's reputation and I'm not taking any chances. That's why I'm letting you know now.'

There was a little pause.

Mr. Usher said, 'No, you'd better be at the office. Get in one or two suitable men to handle the situation if you think you'll need to do that. There isn't much sense in running away from him, Becker. You can't keep away from the office forever. He's bound to come back. Be there tomorrow.' There was a finality in his voice.

'What do I tell him?'

'You know nothing, therefore you can tell him nothing.'

Becker licked his dry lips. 'I don't like it, Mr. Usher.'

'I don't like it much myself,' Mr. Usher admitted coldly, 'but it is a situation with which you will require to cope. You can get the necessary men?'

'Yes, I can get them.' Becker was not enthusiastic. He was less enthusiastic when the line clicked and died in his hand. He laid down the receiver and sat staring at the shuttered window beside him, and he was still so doing when he heard the first low moaning sounds of life in the ante-room. He opened a drawer, drew out a bottle and two glasses and, crossing to the door, turned the key. He turned the handle and stepped into the ante-room.

Ludovic Saxon put one big hand on his chest and pushed him back. 'We'll continue our conversation, Harry,' he said blithely. He turned the key behind him and looked around. 'What's all this? A bottle of Teacher's and two glasses. You expected me back?'

Becker went to his chair behind the desk in silence.

The Picaroon sat at one end of it. 'We'll dispense with the hospitality, Becker,' and now all the flippancy had left his voice and it was cold and hard. 'I was behind the door listening when you made your report. Who is Usher?

'Friend of mine,' Becker said. Wildly he tried to recall

how much of the conversation the Picaroon would have been likely to hear. 'I—I thought I might pick up something from him, Mr. Saxon. About this fellow Lockwood, I mean.'

The Picaroon was in no mood for evasion. 'I know what you mean. Could it be that this friend of yours, this Usher who gives you advice is Simon Usher?' He leaned over Becker now. 'Simon Usher of Smail and Usher?'

Becker nodded. 'That's right, Mr. Saxon. He's been doing some work for me recently.' He made a little motion with his plump hands. 'Income tax. He's a lawyer.'

'He was a lawyer,' the Picaroon said. 'The Bar Association turfed him out ten years ago. The Usher whose name appears in the name of the firm is a nephew who's been in a home for alcoholics for the past seven years. Simon Usher acts as a clerk—Norton Usher is the only qualified lawyer in the partnership.'

Harry Becker made a final attempt. 'There's Smail,' he began. 'I don't—'

'Smail's been retired for years. He's ninety if he's a day.' Ludovic put a large brown hand on Becker's shoulder. 'You fellows never give up. You told him I'd been asking about Lockwood. Why?'

Becker shifted uneasily. 'I was afraid, Mr. Saxon. That's why!'

'You've got reason to be afraid,' the Picaroon said. 'What's your interest in Lockwood?'

Becker gave up the ghost. 'None at all. I don't know the fellow. Never saw him in my life, but Mr. Usher is the man who pays the rent. I have to tell him all that happens here. All of it.' There was a film of perspiration on his forehead. 'I'm not telling the tale, Mr. Saxon. I've heard too much about you. I'm not mixing myself up with anybody your weight.'

'But you still had to report?'

'That's right. Mr. Usher is the man who pays the rent.'

The Picaroon looked down at him pensively. 'True or false, Harry boy?'

'True. It's as true as I'm sitting here.'

'It had better be,' Ludovic said. 'What did Usher say?'

A bead of perspiration broke on Becker's forehead, glissaded down his brow and dropped on to the blotter in front of him. He put up a puffy hand and wiped his forehead with a silk handkerchief. 'He told me to get in one or two boys to handle things when you came back tomorrow.'

The Picaroon nodded. This was very likely to be true. 'Which you were no doubt going to do, Harry boy?'

Becker looked at the whisky. 'Mind if I have a drink?'

'Go ahead,' the Picaroon told him.

Becker poured out a large glass, sipped at it for a moment, then looked up. 'I said I would, but I didn't like it, Mr. Saxon.' He shrugged his shoulders. 'When the boss says you do something, you do it.'

'You've got a point,' Ludovic agreed. 'What about Lockwood?'

'I've told you, I don't know him. I never heard of him before. You asked me about him. I told Mr. Usher.'

For a long moment Ludovic stared down at him. 'I hope you're telling the truth, Becker. If you're not, I'll blind you.' He swung round and walked to the door. When he reached it, he looked back. 'Spahn is beginning to move a limb or two. It might be a good idea to fix transport to take him home, if he has a home.' He closed the door and went down to the street.

At the entranceway, he stood for a moment, listening but there was no sound of a door opening behind him. He stepped out into the road, and walked briskly along to the big black Jaguar which was drawn up a hundred yards away.

MacNab looked round as he appeared. 'You took your time. I was just preparing to go up and look about to see that everything was in order when you appeared.'

The Picaroon got into the front of the car beside him. 'On your way, Mac.'

'Where do we go this time?'

'Home.'

The big car edged away.

MacNab sighed his relief. 'The best spot I can think of at this time of the night. There is nothing like a bit of an east wind and a shower of sleet to make you appreciate a night at the fire with your boots off. That comfortable, and if you've got a tumbler in your hand with something sensible in it, it's just that much the better.' He drove on confidently through icy streets and the Picaroon sat in silence.

They had all but reached Courtfield Mews when the big man said, 'Did you get anything?'

'A little,' Ludovic said, and told him how little.

MacNab was interested. 'Usher? Simon Usher? I don't know him.'

'He's a disbarred solicitor,' Ludovic said. 'He got into trouble with the Law Society ten years ago or so. They tossed him out.'

'Do you tell me that?' MacNab was surprised. 'He must have been a regular rascal when even the very lawyers themselves couldn't be doing with him. It just lets you see what goes on. What had he been up to?'

'I never heard that.'

'He would have his hand in somebody else's pocket,' MacNab said firmly. 'You can be sure enough about that. Them lawyers can do with watching. What does he do now?'

The Picaroon considered. 'He's supposed to do a bit of clerking for a law firm—Smail and Usher. Smail is retired and for all I know dead. The Usher is a nephew of his own—Norton Usher. He's in a home for alcoholics near Sevenoaks and he's been there for the last three or four years. In effect, Simon Usher is the firm. Norton

Usher appears at the office from time to time, but so far as I know, he doesn't handle any work.'

They halted in front of the garage. MacNab slid out and opened the big, steel roller doors.

The Picaroon got in behind the wheel and drove the car inside. He got out of the car, heaved the doors closed with a sharp clang and saw MacNab make his way towards the door that led to the flat. He followed on and a moment or so more and they were walking through the long hall which led to the sitting-room. He moved into it and switched on the light.

MacNab had carried on through the hall. Now he removed his vast topcoat, hung it on a hanger and reached for a hook. 'Just you give the fire a bit of a poke,' he said. 'I'm for a drop of toddy, myself, as soon as I get my slippers on. There's nothing like it on a cold winter's night. That nourishing.' He made his way to his own bedroom, touched the switch and he had taken one step forward into the room when:

Crack!

The glass from the window disintegrated about him and something like an angry bee sped past his ear.

In a second he was on the floor, creeping towards the window out of range. He had all but reached it when he heard the Picaroon's voice behind him.

'You all right, Mac?'

The big man swore in the Gaelic. He saw the Picaroon's hand come round the edge of the doorway towards the switch.

The light went out.

MacNab edged his way towards the door and out to the hallway. A moment passed and he heard the Picaroon say:

'He was shooting from the roof on the other side of the Mews.'

MacNab was on his feet in the darkness. 'My knees! I never felt the like! It is not the thing for a man of nineteen stone to be crawling about on the hard floor on his knees at my time of life. If I get my hands on him I'll have his heart's blood, I'll assure you. Just you let me get down the stairs and you'll see some fine fun.'

The Picaroon appeared, a shadow at his elbow. 'You'll just stay where you are, Mac. Whoever he is, he's gone by now. Anyway, there could be two of them. We don't want to run into any further trouble,' He moved cannily towards the big sitting-room. 'We'll go in and sit in the darkness and have a drink to steady your nerves a little bit.'

'We'll have the drink all right,' MacNab agreed, 'but there is nothing at all the matter with my nerves the way they are.' He followed the Picaroon into the room. 'I see there's still a bit of a fire.' He poked it to life. 'Just you wait till I get a tumbler or two.' He poured out two drinks in the cheerful glow from the fire. 'That's a bit better. There's going to be an awful draught in my bedroom tonight.'

'You'd better take the spare room,' Ludovic said. 'Get Dixon in first thing tomorrow to fix the window.' He lit a cigarette and sat staring into the heart of the fire.

MacNab lit a comforting pipe. 'How long does this go on, this no light?'

'It might not be a bad idea to let it go on all night,' the Picaroon suggested. 'Keep them guessing.'

'There's a lot in what you say,' the big man agreed. 'Keep who guessing?'

Ludovic laughed softly. 'We'll ask Simon Usher,' he said, 'but we'll do it tomorrow, Mac. I want to sleep on this business.' He finished his drink as he spoke. 'I'm pushing off now. Remember. No lights. Goodnight.' He moved off into the darkness of the hall and when MacNab followed ten minutes later, he was sleeping like a child.

10

It was mid-morning and the Picaroon who had been wakened earlier than usual by the sound of hammering in the near vicinity, had just finished breakfast and was smoking his first cigarette of the day, over a cup of coffee, when he heard the outer door close and the sound of very solid footsteps approaching.

MacNab appeared a moment later, filling his pipe. 'That's that. Dixon's man just finished the job. I had a bit look in the bedroom and a fine like job I'll have clearing up after him. You never get tidy tradesmen nowadays. Such a mess the place is in with bits of glass and bits of putty and shavings of wood. If it was not that we might need him back again before long to put in another window I would teach him a fine lesson. Rub his nose in it.' He sat down and stared across at the Picaroon. 'What do you think of yourself?'

Ludovic lit a second cigarete from the butt of the first. 'I'll look up Usher.'

'How far is that going to get you?'

'We won't know till we try.'

MacNab thought it over. 'I've got a better idea. I'll look up Usher.'

The Picaroon shook his head. 'Nothing doing, Mac. This is something I want to handle myself. It's bigger than it looks. We've got Huth and Lockwood out of circulation. We've had this attempt on your life. If it's Usher, he isn't fooling.'

'You don't think it could be Becker himself?'

Ludovic had already considered and discarded this suggestion. 'I don't. Becker's been on the fringe for a long time now, but he's never had the reputation of using violence. Not personally. I can't see him using it now.' He crossed to the table on which the telephone rested, sat down in front of it and lifted the receiver. He began to dial a number, then, when he was through, 'Ludovic Saxon here. Put me on to Peter Saltmarsh.'

Saltmarsh came on a moment later. 'Good morning, Ludovic.'

'It is indeed,' Ludovic said. 'Sleet and snow. You heard what the Met. man said, I trust. Let us not discuss the weather.'

'What do you want to discuss?'

'Trouble. It happened last night. Listen.' He gave a brisk account of the events of the previous evening and when he had finished Saltmarsh said:

'Shot at you from the roof, did he?'

'He shot at Mac.'

'It's a wonder to me he missed him. There's an awful lot of MacNab. Anyway, he means business.'

'So do I,' Ludovic said. 'First of all, I want you to put a useful man on the girl—Mally Huth. Can you do that?'

'You think it necessary?'

'I think it's highly necessary. Huth has disappeared. So has Lockwood. Mac was shot at. There's no reason why whoever is responsible shouldn't take a cut at the girl. Put a good man on her.'

'You've got her address?'

'She lives at 29 Eldridge Walk, Hampstead.' He looked down at the list she had given him. 'She works with Miles and Frensham at 147–158 Wickham Road. I'll get through to her and tell her what we propose to do.'

'Ring me when you've done so.'

'I shall,' Ludovic said. 'There's something else, Peter. What do you know about a bogus old lawyer called Simon Usher?'

'Usher?' Peter Saltmarsh sounded grim. 'I've heard plenty about him. He's been hovering on the borderline for years now.'

'The Law Society put the boot in ten years ago,' Ludovic said. 'I know all that. What I want to know is his rating is at the moment.'

Saltmarsh laughed. 'You're not the only one. The police have had their eye on him for years. They've never been able to do a thing about it. The old man is smooth as velvet. Never puts a foot wrong. Ostensibly, he's only a clerk in the employ of the firm. In fact he is the firm, although you couldn't prove that. You do know about this relation of his—Norton Usher?'

'A cousin, isn't he?'

'It's a little further removed than that,' Saltmarsh said. 'In fact he's the son of a second cousin. Quite a young fellow. I question if he's thirty. In any event he's a dipsomaniac and he spends most of his time in a private nursing home near Sevenoaks. Every now and then, Usher sends a car for him and he appears at the office for a day or two. Ostensibly again, old Usher is acting under his instructions, but that fools no one, though you'd find it hard to get proof. What do you want to do about Usher?'

'I want you to dig a little,' Ludovic said. 'I'll have a word with him.'

'You won't find him an easy man to deal with.'

'I'm not so easy myself,' the Picaroon said. 'He interests me strangely, Peter. I'm going to hang up now. I'll call Mally Sheldon. Call you when I've spoken to her.' He laid down the receiver and looked over at MacNab. 'It begins to look interesting, Mac. Usher is a fake, but how big a fake?' He began to dial again. When a crisp voice said: 'Miles and Frensham. Can I help you?' he said, 'You can indeed. I want to speak to Mrs. Huth.'

The girl came on a moment later. 'Mally Huth speaking.'

'Good morning,' said the Picaroon. 'Ludovic Saxon.'

'Ludovic, have you got something?'

'Just a bit of advice for you.'

'Oh!' She sounded disappointed. 'I thought perhaps that you'd heard something.'

'We shall,' Ludovic said. 'Meantime, what I want to say is this. Your Larry has disappeared. So, unfortunately, has Jack Lockwood.' He heard her draw in her breath.

'Jack Lockwood! But why?'

'That's what we have to find out. My guess is that he discovered something and—'

'You mean about Larry?'

'Yes, it would have to be.'

'But Jack Lockwood gave up the search, Ludovic. I showed you his letter. He made it quite plain.'

'He didn't write it,' Ludovic said. 'I've done a little bit of work on it since I saw you, old girl, and your Larry has stepped into something. He disappeared. You put Lockwood on to it and now he's disappeared.'

There was a little silence, then, 'What do you mean?'

'He hasn't been at the office for a couple of days. He hasn't been at his bed-sitter. I went round to Earls Court to check up on him. Last night, we got into a little bit of trouble ourselves. Under the circumstances, the sensible thing to do is to take one or two precautions.' He told her what those precautions were to consist of and she was a little surprised.

'A bodyguard, Ludovic? Do you think it's really necessary?'

'I think it highly necessary.'

'But I don't know anything about Larry or Jack Lockwood or—'

'Larry is your husband. You put Lockwood on to the job. Both of them have disappeared. You came along to me with your story and last night the powers of darkness caused Mac a great deal of inconvenience.' He laughed softly. 'Tell you about it some other time. Anyway, I've arranged you'll have someone around just in case. If you went a.w.o.l., it would mess things up for everyone.'

'I suppose you're right.'

'In this kind of thing I'm always right,' Ludovic said. 'Well, nearly always. Expect to see a large and good looking young man hovering around you from now on. I'll tell Peter to hand-pick him. Seriously, just be a bit more careful for a few days. Whoever these people are, they mean business. Agreed?'

'Yes, I suppose you know best.'

'How right you are,' the Picaroon said. He hung up.

MacNab was clearing away the coffee pot and dishes. 'Everything in order?'

'It is,' Ludovic said. 'She wasn't too keen on the idea at first. Funny how a woman's first instinct is to argue, Mac, as soon as you tell her about anything.'

'It's the truth,' MacNab said solemnly. 'Have I not often noticed it myself? Man, was I not nearly married to one myself when I was a young fellow up on Loch Aline. As nice a girl as you would meet and, thinks I, I'll just hang up my hat with her while I'm in the mood, and save a lot of trouble looking around later for someone else.'

'And what happened?' asked Ludovic, interested.

MacNab sighed. 'I had just started a job at the keeping at the time and there was as nice a wee house went with it as ever you saw, so, thinks I, I'll tell her about the house first and work my way round to the other thing gradual like, and that's what I did, but we never got any further than the road up to the house itself. Her father and her two brothers had worked on it, and I happened to say, just by way of general conversation, that the road up to the sheiling wasn't a very good road and that finished it. Take you what I got. We spent an hour talking about the road with me never opening my mouth again. So that was that and I never said another word about an engagement. A narrow escape. My goodness, but it taught me a lesson, I'll assure you.'

'That was something,' Ludovic said and began to dial again. A moment later Saltmarsh was on the line, and he said, 'Ludovic here, Peter. I've spoken to Mally Huth, She understands the situation. Put someone good on the job. I want a watch round the clock.'

'I can manage it. I've arranged for Tempest to take her home tonight. He'll call at the office. He's a reliable fellow. I'll attend to the details myself.'

'Good man,' Ludovic said. He made an assignation for three o'clock, hung up and looked round. 'That's fixed, Mac.'

'What happens now?'

Ludovic looked thoughtful. 'We do a bit of checking.'

'Usher?'

'Usher,' agreed the Picaroon malignantly, and went through to dress for the occasion.

11

Since it was not in Ludovic Saxon's nature to let events take charge of him, he lunched at The Marchester and withdrew to smoke off the effects of it in the Marigold Room.

Peter Saltmarsh arrived at exactly three o'clock, a small slight figure in a well-worn trench-coat, and few would have imagined that this unimpressive little man was one of the smartest private operators in the Kingdom. He came in briskly, crossed to the corner in which the Picaroon, sunk in the depths of a large armchair could vaguely be seen, and tapped him on the knee. 'Waken up, princess.'

'Sit down, Peter.'

Saltmarsh took off his coat, tossed it on an adjacent chair and sat down.

The Picaroon leaned back and touched a bell. When the waiter arrived, he said, 'Beer. Two pints.' When it was brought and the man had gone, he produced cigarettes.

'Did you get anything?'

Saltmarsh shook his head. 'I didn't, and I question if you'll get hold of anything either. None of them can give me anything concrete at all. Each of them says Usher is on the hook, but you'll never prove it. He's as wide as Broad Street.'

'He made a mistake once,' Ludovic said, 'and they jumped him for it.'

'He did. I've inquired about that. As far as I can find out the mistake wasn't made by him. It was made by his clerk. And it was his association who came down on him—not the police. The way I heard it they'd been watching for an opportunity and this was too good a chance to miss.' He smiled grimly. 'A lot of different people have tried to get him, Ludovic.'

'A tough baby!'

'You could say that.'

'Take a look at me,' the Picaroon said. 'You see a tougher.' He changed the subject. 'You've made your arrangements about protection for Mally Huth.'

'Yes. Tempest is taking it in hand. I've arranged for Lynn Tully to sleep with her at her flat. Tempest will have a shakedown in the hall. Mrs. Huth says they've got a camp bed she can dig out for him. Tempest will escort her to her office in the morning then catch up on some sleep. He'll pick her up again at five-thirty, which is when she leaves the office.'

'She didn't make any trouble about it?'

'No, she was quite co-operative. I got Lynn to speak to her.' Saltmarsh looked at his watch. 'I've got to get back soon, Ludovic. I'm having a busy afternoon.'

The Picaroon shook his head. 'I don't know how you do it?'

'What else is there to do?' Peter Saltmarsh said grimly. 'We can't all be self-indulgent mortals like you, Ludovic. Some of us have to work for a living.' He hesitated. 'If you do go along to have a word with Usher, be careful what you say to him if you're in his office.'

'You think there may be witnesses in the offing?'

'I wasn't exactly thinking of witnesses,' Saltmarsh confessed. 'More of tape-recorders.'

'I'll remember it.'

'Anyway his office staff don't amount to much. There's a woman—a Miss Prosser who does the Income Tax for him and his typing. There's an old clerk, Carraccini, who potters around the office and seems to be the office boy.'

'Italian?'

'In fact, no. He's third generation English. His great-grandfather came over here in the mid-eighties.'

'You've done your homework,' Ludovic said.

'I put Darby on to it,' Saltmarsh said. 'You have to have facts.'

'What facts have you got on the secretary woman?'

'Amy Prosser? She's forty-four, plain, sallow, grey hair and single. She lives in a flat at 29, Mallow Court, Chelsea. In case you think that sounds a toney address, the flat consists of a kitchenette, a bedroom, bathroom and sitting-room. It costs her two hundred and eighty pounds a year. You will gather that it is not sumptuous.' Saltmarsh smiled. 'She's an efficient worker. She's been with Usher for about six years now. If you're interested, she's a Canadian.'

'What about Usher himself?'

'Sixty-four. He lives in a big old-fashioned semi-detached at Golders Green. He has a manservant to look after him, Mark Kilby. Kilby has been with him for years. The address is Modder, Seldon Road, Golders Green.'

'That dates the house,' Ludovic said.

Peter Saltmarsh nodded. 'I suppose it does. That's all I've got.' He rose abruptly. 'Got to go now, Ludovic. As I said I've got a heavy day ahead of me yet.' He drew on his coat, tightened the belt round his narrow waist and frowned down at the Picaroon. 'I don't feel too comfortable about this business, Ludovic. If you've got it right, Huth and Lockwood have both vanished and someone tried to shoot you up last night. I hadn't imagined that Usher would attempt violence, but—'

'I don't think Usher will, but he'll know the men to use.'

'Same thing,' Saltmarsh said. 'Just watch it, Ludovic, because his record is that he's a very wily character indeed. Ring me later and tell me what comes out of the interview.'

'I'll do that,' said the Picaroon and watched him leave. When Saltmarsh had gone, he smoked a final cigarette, rose and made his way down to the front doors of The Marchester and when a taxi was summoned, climbed into it. When the driver looked round at him : 'Lyman's Hotel, Meeching Street.'

'Very good, sir.'

Lyman's Hotel was situate within five minutes' walk of the Cromwell Road. He was deposited in front of its quiet, even genteel front door, and made his way into the foyer and past the reception desk with all the assurance of a man who had been there many times before.

The ancient clerk looked up and nodded to him in silence.

The Picaroon returned his salutation and sought the self-operated lift. He took this to the fourth floor and when he left it, walked along a narrow corridor to a room at the rear of the hotel. On the door was the simple designation 48. He produced a key and let himself inside, locking the door behind him.

It was a small room with a single tall window. He crossed over and drew the blind, and when he was satisfied, he switched on a side light. He removed his topcoat, tossing it on to the bed, and when he had done so, he crossed to the built-in wardrobe, produced a key from his pocket and opened the door.

Inside, on hangers, was an array of clothing. He chose a suit of a dark, chocolate brown, well worn, shiny in the proper places, and somewhat scuffed at the foot of the trouser legs. With it, he selected a slightly crumpled shirt, cream-coloured, but with a large brown check, a red necktie and a brown pork-pie hat.

He donned the shirt and trousers, then sat down in front of the dressing-table, touched a switch and a tubular bar above the mirror lit up. The Picaroon produced a little make-up box and went to work with the skill of an artist. It was rarely that Ludovic Saxon affected a disguise. When he did so, he became the man he set out to be. For half an hour he worked carefully on his features, touched up his dark, crisp hair so that it became shot with grey and lank and soft. He fitted a gold shell on a front tooth, and washed his face with a mild solution of annatta so that when he was finished, his appearance was jaded and sallow.

Now he let the solution dry on his hands, soiled his finger-nails and knotted the red necktie round his neck. From the bottom of the wardrobe, he drew a pair of scuffed brown shoes, pulled them on and tied the laces slackly. He drew on the waistcoat and jacket, put a pair of horn-rimmed glasses on his nose and donned the hat. For a moment or so he surveyed himself in the mirror, using the side mirrors to check from every angle, then picking up a soiled green raincoat, he left the room and made his way downstairs.

The ancient clerk was still toiling at the reception

desk. He did not look up and the Picaroon stepped out into the fading light of a December afternoon. He made his way along to the Underground, took a ticket to Camden Town and made his way slowly down to train level.

It was half-past four now. He travelled to Camden Town, a stooped and dismal-looking individual, who might have been a clerk in some dreary and paltry establishment. He walked round to Minton Street, and noted with interest that the entrance to it was opposite a small tea shop. Thirty yards beyond the tea shop and on the same side was a telephone kiosk. He walked along to the kiosk, inserted a coin and dialled the number of that firm of legal luminaries, Smail and Usher. For a moment or so he listened to the sound of the buzzer at the other end, then came a little click.

'Smail and Usher.' It was a woman's voice.

The Picaroon coughed. 'Afternoon, miss. It's Mr. Usher I want.'

'Who's speaking please?'

'Name of Dyson. Tod Dyson. You won't know me, miss, nor Mr. Usher either. I got into a little bit of bother the other day and a guy I met said I should look up Mr. Usher. You think he could see me just now?'

There was a little silence.

'I'm not certain,' she said. 'Mr. Usher is here just now. I'll ask him to speak to you, Mr. Dyson, you said?'

'Yes, ma'am.'

'And your address?'

'From Canada. You can tell him Montreal. That's where I was last. I've been around a bit though. Toronto, Hamilton, London, Hull, Windsor and quite a lot more places.'

'I'll tell him that,' she said. 'Hold on a moment please.'

He could hear the sound of her rapid footsteps as she moved away.

Presently she returned. 'Mr. Usher has a client with

74

him just now, Mr. Dyson. I wasn't aware of that when I spoke to you. Normally he would be leaving the office at this time, but he is prepared to see you. Can you be here by five-thirty?'

'Yeah, I can manage that.'

'Very good. I shall let Mr. Usher know to expect you. Good afternoon.' She hung up.

The Picaroon did likewise and walked along to the tea shop. He went inside, took a seat which commanded a view of the window, ordered a cup of tea and a cake. When he had been supplied with it, he ate the cake, lit a cigarette and sat back to wait.

The building across from him gradually emptied, and when the hands of his watch were at five twenty-five, he pushed aside his cup, pressed out the butt of his cigarette in the saucer and left the shop.

Two minutes later he was on the narrow stairway of 64 Minton Street. He made his way up to the second floor, and on the first door to confront him he read:

SMAIL & USHER

Solicitors

The Picaroon turned the handle and went inside.

12

There was a short counter as he entered the door, and on the other side an unpretentious general office in which a grey-haired woman was working at a desk which was piled high with ledgers of various sizes, bits of brown wrapping-paper along with crushed lengths of corrugated paper, and by this token, the Picaroon recognised Miss Prosser who did the Income Tax work for Mr. Usher.

She was doing it now. There was a hateful buff form spread out in front of her and she was moving a pencil down this from one line to another.

The Picaroon coughed. 'Evening, miss.'

She looked round almost in surprise. 'Oh, yes. Mr. Dyson?'

'That's it, miss.'

She looked up at the clock. 'Mr. Usher should be ready for you now.' She rose as she spoke. 'I'll find out for you.' She went through a doorway, closing it behind her. When she returned a moment later she said, 'Mr. Usher will see you in five minutes. Just sit down, Mr. Dyson.'

There were two ancient basket chairs at the far end of the counter. The Picaroon sat down on the nearer one.

Miss Prosser had gone back to her desk, but she was not entirely without curiosity. 'You said you had been in Canada?'

'That's right, miss, I just got here last week.

'But you're not a Canadian?'

The Picaroon agreed that such was the case. 'Not me. Liverpool born and bred. Been around a bit though.' His voice sharpened. 'You sound like you've been in Canada yourself, miss.'

She nodded. 'Yes, I was born there. Chatham. It's quite a small place. In Ontario. It's about halfway between Windsor and London.'

'I know it,' Ludovic said. 'Been there often, miss. The kind of job I had kept me on the road a lot. You had to pass through Chatham. You been there recently?'

'Not for twenty years.'

'You wouldn't know the place now.'

76

'I don't suppose I would,' she agreed.

'You come here after the war?'

She nodded. 'Yes. With a friend. She went back to Montreal. I was enjoying life and I stayed on. I've never gone back.' She half-smiled. 'Some day, I shall.' She stood staring down at her desk, then crossed to a door, opened it and took out a green tweed coat. She drew it on, arranged her hat and smiled at him. 'I usually leave the office at half past five, Mr. Dyson. I waited tonight because you were a Canadian. I'll see if Mr. Usher is ready for you now.' She went back through the doorway, to reappear in a moment.

'Yes. Will you just come this way?'

He followed her through to a little corridor which had a door which must have led to the hallway outside. Through this, Mr. Usher's client must have made his way, for when she ushered him into the room, there was only the lawyer himself.

Miss Prosser said, 'Mr. Dyson, Mr. Usher.' She smiled at the Picaroon. 'Goodnight.'

'Goodnight,' the lawyer said.

The door closed behind her.

There was a chair in front of the desk. Simon Usher pointed to it. 'Sit down, Mr. Dyson.'

The Picaroon did so and looked across the desk with interest.

Simon Usher was a tall, thin man in his mid-sixties. He had a high forehead with a crop of whitish hair brushed backwards, a pendulous nose and thin bloodless lips. His features were lean and gaunt, his eyes pale blue and ice hard. He watched the Picaroon for a moment, then, 'Miss Prosser tells me you have an—um— problem of some sort.'

'That's right,' said Ludovic.

Simon Usher was not impressed. 'First of all, who sent you here?' He placed the tips of his long bony fingers together and watched the Picaroon.

'Joe Prideaux!'

Simon Usher's eyes flickered faintly. 'And who is Joe Prideaux?'

'A guy I know in Montreal.' The Picaroon leaned forward 'O.K., Mr. Usher, maybe you don't know him, but you could pretty soon find out about him if you're interested. Anyway, he knows you, and when I had to come over here, he rang me up. "Look, Tod," he says, "you go over to England, you can do with a bit of help. There ain't a lot of openings in your line of business." That's what he said.' He looked over at the lawyer.

'O.K. He had something there and I'm the first man to admit it. Maybe I have got a kind of specialised line. Anyway, I said, "What have you got in mind, Joe?" Well, he told me. "You want to get fixed up, go see a guy called Simon Usher. He's a lawyer. Got an office in Minton Street. Look him up when you get to London." ' Ludovic shrugged. 'So that's it. I'm here. I'm looking you up. Joe says you can probably do something for me. What do you think?'

There was a little silence.

'Miss Prosser had a different story.'

'Not so much different,' the Picaroon said. 'She just got an outline. You don't expect I'm going to tell my life story to the help.'

Usher watched him unblinkingly. 'What is your line of business?'

The Picaroon smiled a thin, twisted little smile. 'You could say I was a bit of a trouble-shooter.' He expanded it a little. 'If there was a bit of trouble, I did a bit of shooting.'

'Where was this?'

Ludovic looked at him craftily. 'Here and there. I've worked in Detroit, Chicago, Montreal. I did one or two little jobs for Prideaux in Montreal.' He thought for a moment. 'Tell you something, Mr. Usher. I slipped out of line once or twice. Usually it don't matter too much.

78

The law don't worry a lot about an odd dead gunman lying about here and there. Saves them trouble. Cops don't like trouble any more than business men like Joe Prideaux like them. You know why? Because they have to run around and do a bit of cleaning up.' He rubbed his big strong hands together.

'All right, I stepped out of line and that wasn't my fault altogether. They told me I had to hit this guy who who would be sitting in a green Chrysler in front of the Red Thorn Tree around eleven o'clock. Well, I was there at eleven o'clock. So was he and I hit him.' He scowled at Usher. 'Only he turned out to be a cop. You know what that means. I had to get out and quick.'

Simon Usher said, 'Go on.'

'Well, Joe got me out. I had to come here. Liverpool. I can't go back. Joe knows that, so he says, "See this lawyer, Usher." That's all.'

There was a long silence. A clock ticked on the mantelshelf and the Picaroon was suddenly aware that outside, the light had disappeared and that particles of sleet were chattering at the window.

Simon Usher leaned forward. 'I don't know this man Prideaux.'

'He didn't say you did. He said that you were the man to see. That's why I'm here.'

'How did you get out of Montreal?'

'Boat,' Ludovic said. 'It wasn't so easy.'

'What ship?'

'It wasn't a liner. A damn old tub, the *Tambourlaine*. She's registered in Panama—6,000 gross. Cargo and what she could pick up where she touched. The master was a Greek. Joe figured it. It cost him something. I never heard how much. They treated me pretty good, but she was a tub for all that. We got into Liverpool a week ago.'

'Is she still there?'

'She sailed on Friday,' the Picaroon said. 'I don't know where. They were a pretty mixed lot. Greek, Italian,

German and a couple of Swedes, and some coloured crew. The quartermaster was an Irishman from Sligo. He said something about Antwerp and then on to the Med. That's all I know.'

'And what do you want me to do?'

Ludovic shrugged. 'You know somebody who can fix me up in a job, you've got a good man. I'm saying that myself. It's up to you, mister, but I have to get an answer of some kind. Yes or no?'

Simon Usher stared at him impassively. 'Let us get something straight, Dyson. You've been in the States for how long?'

'Seven years.'

'And you've been acting as a—a—'

'Bodyguard,' the Picaroon suggested. 'Some say one thing, some say another. Bodyguard sounds as good as any of them.'

Usher nodded. 'As a bodyguard. You tell me you killed a policeman in Montreal and that this man Prideaux helped you to get away by sea and suggested you come to me. I am correct, am I not?'

The Picaroon nodded. 'That's it, Mr. Usher. Joe said you could probably fix things up. What do you think?'

Simon Usher smiled a cold, thin-lipped smile. 'I think I'd be very foolish indeed to mix myself up in such a matter.'

'So you're not interested?'

'Not personally,' Simon Usher said, With a long, white forefinger he stroked his nose. 'At the same time, it might be possible that something could be done for you. But before anything is done, I should have to get in touch with this man Prideaux in Montreal.'

Ludovic nodded. 'That's fair enough. You want his address?'

The lawyer pushed across a sheet of paper and a desk pen. 'Write it there.'

The Picaroon arranged the paper in front of him and

lifted the pen. He turned it over in his fingers once or twice, then began to write.

Joe Prideaux, Apartment 2, Armande Terrace, Peletier Street, Montreal.

He stared at what he had written for a moment or two then pushed it across.

Usher read it over. 'Do you know his telephone number?'

'Yeah.' Ludovic reached over and began to jot it down.

Simon Usher stared at him unblinkingly. 'I am making no promises, Mr. Dyson, but I shall investigate this. It may be that I shall be able to pass your name along to someone who can be useful to you. I have an—um— client, who might find a use for you. You understand, I make no promise.'

The Picaroon nodded. 'Sure, Mr. Usher.'

'And what about your present address?'

The Picaroon shook his head. 'No dice, Mr. Usher. I don't talk about that. You know why? Because maybe I go back there tonight and find a whole raft of cops waiting for me. So I don't tell. Not till we get to know each other better.'

The lawyer nodded. For the first time there was a faint flicker in his cold eyes. 'Quite so. But if I have to trust you, that trust has to be mutual.'

Ludovic shook his head. 'Not so, Mr. Usher. I'm not asking you to trust me with your life. You know what happens if I've squirrelled thing up? The law take me and ship me back to Montreal. They still hang you in Quebec, especially if you kill a cop. Not for me.'

Simon Usher nodded. 'As you say. You keep in touch. Ring me at the office here, tomorrow night at six o'clock. I am always here at that time and I am alone. My staff has gone. You understand?'

'Sure,' the Picaroon said. He cleared his throat. 'There's one thing more, Mr. Usher. I came away short. Right now I've got eleven pounds. That don't go all that far.'

'You mean you want me to advance you money?'

'Fix me up and you get it back.'

Mr. Usher opened a drawer in his desk at his hand. He lifted out a black-japanned money box, unlocked it and lifted out five five-pound notes. He laid it on the desk in front of him. 'There you are. Twenty-five pounds, Mr. Dyson. I shall expect to get it back.'

'Sure,' the Picaroon said. He lifted the notes. 'Good of you, Mr. Usher. I figured Joe knew what he was talking about.' He placed the money in a narrow, yellow wallet, and as he did so, Simon Usher was able to see the backs of two or three orange-coloured bills. He watched the Picaroon restore the wallet to his pocket and when he had done so, the Picaroon buttoned up his coat.

'That's all, Mr. Usher. I'll ring you tomorrow night at six o'clock.' He rose as he spoke.

Simon Usher had risen too. Now he escorted him to the door, opened it and led him along the narrow hall to the door he had already noticed. There was a mortise lock with a heavy key in the lock. The lawyer turned the key and opened the door. He looked out into the feeble light of the outer passageway. 'Goodnight to you, Mr. Dyson.'

'Goodnight,' said the Picaroon. He stepped out and the door closed behind him. He made his way silently down to the street and to the shower of sleet which the chill nor' easter bore in its teeth. He made his way along to the underground station at Camden Town, took a ticket for Earls Court and spent an hour changing trains and waiting in draughty stations before he arrived at Meeching Street. Here he went into Lyman's Hotel and took the lift to the fourth floor and to the privacy of his room.

It was half an hour later that he emerged, locked

the door and made his way to the ground floor. He passed out into the darkness of the night and a quarter of an hour later was fitting his key into the lock of the flat in Courtfield Mews.

13

MacNab was sitting by the fire in the sitting-room, a pipe in his mouth and in his hand a copy of *Kenilworth*. He was the only person the Picaroon knew who still read Scott, and he regarded him with admiration. 'I see you're still at it, Mac. You're a glutton for punishment.'

MacNab took the pipe out of his mouth. 'Ach, I don't know. There's body in it. Body. When you're reading Scott you've got something to get your teeth into. And character too. They had character—whether it was good or bad. Look at yon fellow Varney!' He shook his head and laid the book aside. 'How did you get on?'

'I saw Usher.'

'What do you think?'

'He's as bent as your elbow,' Ludovic said. He sat down, lit a cigarette and sighed. 'I could do with a pint, Mac, if you're having something yourself.'

MacNab was ever the soul of hospitality. 'What am I thinking of? It's all this reading I'm doing. Making me forgetful.' He went through to the kitchen for beer, brought it and poured out a drink from a decanter for himself. 'I'll just have a dram. All that beer is not good for anybody.' He sampled it. 'What happened?'

'Listen,' the Picaroon said, and told him.

MacNab gave him close attention. 'You took a chance.'

'You have to take chances,' Ludovic said.

'He'll check up on you.'

'I'll put through a call to Joe Prideaux in Montreal at once. Joe will back me up all right. In any event it was the easiest way to get Usher to show his hand.'

'I don't know that I like it,' MacNab objected. 'You knew he was bent before you started. You could just have let it go at that.'

Ludovic took a pull at the pewter pot he held in his hand. 'I heard he was bent, Mac. I heard it on every hand. But I didn't know it. Now I do.'

'And what's going to come out of that?'

'We'll wait and see.'

MacNab puffed thoughtfully at his pipe. 'Maybe yes and maybe no. You could get an awful surprise, and it's me that's telling you.'

The Picaroon laid down his beer and moved across to the telephone, lifted the receiver, and began to dial. 'I'm going to book a call to Joe.'

MacNab sat in pensive silence as the preliminaries were gone through. When the Picaroon had laid down the receiver again, the big man said: 'If Usher is as smart as they say he is, he's going to have his doubts about you. My goodness, but he is! What do you think your-self?'

'Perhaps,' the Picaroon said. His grey eyes were dancing. 'You know me, Mac, go to the top every time. See the boss and size him up. Don't be fobbed off with second raters and underlings. Besides, it was worth it.'

'What do you mean?'

Ludovic looked at him dreamily. 'I made a discovery.'

'About Usher?'

'About Usher,' Ludovic agreed, 'and that discovery, Mac, my ancient oatmeal savage, was worth any chance I may have taken. If I hadn't gone up to see old Usher I shouldn't have made it, but I did and I have. My luck is in. This I consider a good and fair omen. Give me luck every time. Especially good luck.'

MacNab was coldly sceptical. 'I don't hold with luck. I was brought up to put my faith in hard work and getting up in the morning. When it comes to omens it's not a word I like to hear at all, at all.' He shook his head in reproof.

'The Romans believed in them,' Ludovic pointed out. 'Never took a decision, Mac, without checking up on the entrails of an owl. When those bright old chaps thought omens worth while, who are we to have other ideas?'

MacNab laid down his pipe. 'Entrails of an owl! Man, but I wonder at you. What kind of talk is that in a Christian household?'

The Picaroon laughed. 'It worked, Mac. That's what I'm interested in. Now I'm going to ring Mally Sheldon.' He crossed to the telephone and put through a call. When he heard the girl's voice, 'Ludovic Saxon here.'

'I wondered if you'd call.'

'You can expect me to,' the Picaroon said. 'I understand you've got company.'

'Lynn is a pet, and Geoffrey is a darling.'

The Picaroon had never thought of Tempest in those precise terms. 'I don't know. A bit on the massive side for a darling, isn't he?'

'You know what I mean.' She changed the subject abruptly. 'Ludovic, have you got anything yet?'

'I'm making a little progress,' he said cautiously. 'It isn't done quickly.' He thought for a moment. 'You said your husband seemed a bit elated for a few days before he disappeared?'

'Yes, I'm certain of it now. I've been thinking about that since you spoke of it yesterday and I'm certain you're right about it. Larry was usually pretty self-contained. In fact, he was one of the calmest people I've ever met. He was never flustered or upset but for those few days I'm certain he was disturbed about something.'

85

'Think carefully. Pleasantly or unpleasantly?'

'I couldn't say—just excited as much as he could be excited.'

'And he didn't give you a clue to the cause of it?'

'I'm afraid he didn't. As I say, he never talked about his work.'

'Well, think about it,' the Picaroon said. 'If you remember anything, let me know.'

'I'll do that.'

'Fine,' he said. 'I'll leave you to your friends. Sleep well.' He hung up, came back and lit a cigarette.

MacNab watched him shrewdly. 'You've got an idea?'

'It's so faint you couldn't even call it that, Mac.'

'They all begin that way,' MacNab said. 'Just you take a dram and sit back with your eyes shut and it will come to you all the sooner. I know what I'm talking about. Many's the time I've tried it.'

The Picaroon shook his head. 'I'll think without the dram, Mac.'

'It's a great mistake,' MacNab cautioned. 'The very worst thing you could do, and it's me that's got my eye on you. Just you take a small dram and think things over. That's my advice to you.'

The Picaroon yawned. 'A small one then, Mac. I'm weakening.'

MacNab who, far from considering the drinking of spirits a weakness was of the school which regarded it as the underpinnings of strength and vigour, rose to dispense the prescription. 'I'll just take the same myself, to keep you company. The solitary drinking is a bad bad thing for anyone. It gets to be a habit and then where are you?' He laid down a glass at Ludovic's hand.

'Just you drink that up and close your eyes and think. You'll find yourself with some of the finest thoughts a man ever had, I'm telling you.'

The Picaroon sat back, carried out the full treatment

86

and pondered and he was still pondering when the telephone rang.

It was MacNab who answered it. He looked round abruptly. 'It's your call to Joe Prideaux.'

The Picaroon moved across to take the receiver.

There was a little delay, then came the voice of Joe Prideaux, an ancient ally. 'Hullo, Ludovic. That you?'

'In person. How are you, Joe?'

'Fat as a porker,' Prideaux said. 'Less a few teeth and some hair since I saw you. I'm getting old, Ludovic. What's on your mind?'

'I want you to do something for me.'

'I figured that. You don't spend money on trans-Atlantic calls unless there's a very good reason for it. Let's hear about it. Just give me time to get the tape recorder.'

The Picaroon let him hear. He spoke briefly and clearly and when he had finished, Joe Prideaux said:

'OK. Let's go over it again. This character Usher is likely to call me and check on your story. You're Tod Dyson. I helped you get away from Montreal when you were in a spot because you shot a cop. That right so far?'

'That's right, Joe.'

'I've got that much. Right, I got you off on a Greek ship, the *Tambourlaine*. The skipper was a Greek too —a pal of mine. If this Usher is smart, he'll want his name.'

'Usher is smart.'

'Right. He was Nick Constantine.'

'He's going to want to know who the policeman was.'

'I can fix that. Felix La Russe. That'll stand up. But I'll hedge on it if I have to. Tell him it don't do to talk about cops getting hit. Anything else?'

'Yes. I told Usher you put me on to him. He wonders how you knew. You can think that one out for yourself, Joe. You wouldn't need to spell it out for me anyway, so that means I don't need to have my own answer.'

Prideaux said, 'We've got half a dozen English hooks here. One of 'em mentioned Usher. It could have been Dolly Barford, it could have been Slaven or the Blue Parrot. I'll get by on that one all right. Any more?'

'That's about all, Joe.'

'O.K.,' Prideaux said. 'I'll fix it. If he still sounds cagey, I'll buzz you tomorrow night maybe. Take care of yourself.'

'Thanks, Joe.'

'O.K.,' Prideaux said and hung up.

The Picaroon laid down his own receiver. 'That's fixed, Mac.'

MacNab nodded aprovingly. 'A fine, hardy chap Joe Prideaux and good company at any time. As cheery as another man's wedding. I had a champion night with him in Quebec when you were in New York. The Château Frontenac! Him and me, and one by the name of Raoul, and a chap Messines, and one or two other gentlemen. Man, but the drink was flowing like water that night, and there were some sore heads in Quebec the next morning, I'll assure you. You never saw a—'

The telephone rang out peremptorily.

'I wonder who it is,' MacNab said irritably. 'A late, late hour of night to be phoning a respectable household.'

The Picaroon had crossed the room. Now he lifted the receiver. 'Ludovic Saxon here.' He heard the sound of forced and rapid breathing, then :

'Saxon!'

'That's right. Who's calling?'

'You won't know me.' The voice was hoarse. 'The name is Lockwood. Jack Lockwood!'

14

For a second Ludovic was startled. 'Jack Lockwood!'

'Yes. You won't know me but Miss Sheldon, that's Mrs. Huth, a—'

'She was here yesterday,' Ludovic said. 'She told me about you. I tried to locate you. I called at your office—I called at your rooms. Where are you now?'

'Just a minute.' There was the sound of the receiver being laid down. The muffled sound of footsteps moving across a wooden floor. A moment later, then the receiver was lifted again. 'Hullo.'

'What happened?'

'I thought I heard someone moving outside,' Lockwood said.

'Where are you?'

'Connelly's Saw Mill.'

'Where's that?'

'Baron Alley, Camden Town,' Lockwood said grimly. 'Look Mr. Saxon, let me do the talking. I've been here for a couple of nights now. Lying close, understand. That's what this job has got me. You know the thing the young lady came to me about.'

'I know. She told me about it. You've found out something?'

'Yes. You could say that. But not much. Just enough to make trouble for myself, Mr. Saxon. You ever hear of Chris Donlevy or Len Kuvelik?'

The Picaroon drew in his breath. 'Donlevy! You mean the Australian crowd who pulled the big gold steal a year or so back?'

'That's the crowd,' Lockwood said. 'I can't talk much longer, see? It just isn't safe. I've been holing up here for the last couple of days or so.'

89

'You know this man Connelly?'

'Yes. He's a friend of mine. I've done him a good turn once or twice. This time I was on the spot and I rang him up. He let me hole up here. It isn't so easy. It isn't a big place. Just employs about a dozen men. I stay up in the attic. It isn't in use, and nobody comes up here. So far I've been lucky. Connelly has managed to hand me in a flask of tea and some sandwiches. But I've got to get out of here, pretty damn soon. It isn't safe.' He swallowed.

'This Donlevy plays it rough, Mr. Saxon. I don't know just what's going on, but whatever it is, it's big. It would have to be big to interest Donlevy. You know what the kill was on the bullion steal. Three-quarters of a million.'

'It was never found,' Ludovic said. 'How did you come across Donlevy?'

'Saw him in Adelaide eight years back,' Lockwood said. 'I was in the Navy then. Donlevy was in the police in those days. I met him once or twice.' He stirred restlessly. 'Look, Mr. Saxon, I reckon I've been here long enough. These boys know I'm on the job. I've got the feeling they've been around. There's a guard dog here, a great damn Alsatian. I heard him growling once or twice. I don't think it was me he heard. It could be, but I can't be sure. Anyway, I want to find a safer place. Miss Mally—that's Mrs. Huth—said she knew you. She said she was going to see if you could help her. She didn't need to tell me too much. I'd heard plenty about you myself. What I want is to get out of here. It has to be soon. Do you think you can help me?'

'I'll lay it on. Baron Alley.'

'It's a dead end,' Lockwood said. 'On your right as you come in. It's an old brick building. One or two car lock-ups before you reach it.'

'What about this dog you spoke about?'

'That's O.K., Mr. Saxon. He's outside only. There's a bit of a shed for him to go into for shelter. He's been restless for the last half hour or so. How long before you can get over?' His voice sounded uneasy.

'Give us half an hour. Where do we get you?'

'I'm in the office just now,' Lockwood said. 'I came down here to use the phone. It wasn't too easy either. I can't show a light. All I've got is a torch with the business end taped. What time do you make it?'

'It's one-thirty-six.'

'I'll set my watch,' Lockwood said. 'I'm seven minutes fast. Right, Mr. Saxon, I'll wait it out here till I hear you come to the front of the workshop. There's an eight or nine foot brick wall with barbed wire on top. There's a big green painted wooden door with a little narrow door set in it. I haven't got a key, so you'll have to throw me a rope or something. I can manage on a rope fine. I won't come out till I hear you because of this damn dog I told you about though. Don't keep me waiting long, because he'll likely bark his damn head off and I don't want to attract any more attention than I can help.'

'I'll bring a rope,' the Picaroon said.

'Right, Mr. Saxon. Good of you, sir.' There was relief in the man's voice.

'Half an hour then,' Ludovic said. 'Goodbye.' He hung up.

MacNab was stolidly putting on his shoes. 'What was all that about?'

'Hurry-up job, Mac. Lockwood. I'll tell you about it on the way. We'll take a coil of rope with us and one or two of Sellar's ampoules.'

MacNab nodded. 'A fine idea. I heard you mention a dog. The ampoules is the very thing for them. That humane.' He stamped to see if his shoes fitted comfortably. 'I'll get the car out.'

'Do so,' said the Picaroon and the big man hurried towards the stairway. He had the car in the lane when the Picaroon appeared to close the big roller doors.

Ludovic got in the car. 'We're going to Connelly's

Saw Mill, Baron Alley in Camden Town. Lockwood's hiding up there.' He sat back and explained the situation as the big man drove through bare deserted streets.

'Hiding out!' MacNab said. 'In a saw mill. A dry like place for the job. It's not me that would hide two or three days among shavings and sawdust, I'll assure you. What's he hiding there for?'

'Do you remember Chris Donlevy?'

MacNab drove on for a second or two. 'Donlevy. Was that not the Australian fellow that was in the bullion robbery a while back?'

'It was. He was an ex-policeman.'

'That's a caper for you,' MacNab said. 'The bullion robbery. More than half a million they took, if I mind right.'

'Three-quarters of a million. It was never recovered. There were no arrests. We were abroad at the time, but there was plenty of talk about it.'

'There were some security men killed,' MacNab said. 'Two of them.'

'That's right. Shot down. Donlevy's crowd used gel-ignite to blast the vans open. There were two vans.' He was silent for a moment or so. 'It begins to make sense, Mac.'

'It's a fact,' MacNab said solemnly. 'Man, do you tell me that this fellow Usher was mixed up in a job of those dimensions?'

'It looks like it.'

They swung into a gloomy, narrow street and MacNab became silent as he concentrated on his directions. A moment or so later he said, 'Fine. I know where we are. Baron Alley is along on the left. It's a cul de sac. What do we do?'

'Drive down to the end and turn,' Ludovic said. 'Lock-wood will be listening for us. He won't come out of the building till he hears us coming. There's a guard dog on the premises, but he doesn't want to tangle with it.'

'And he's right,' MacNab said fiercely. 'Them guard dogs is a devil of a nuisance. I mind fine one at Johnny Durocher's place at Wapping. Spoiled a good pair of trousers on me. You have that ampoule handy.'

They had entered the narrow street. It was short and was lit by only one standard and, at the far end, there was a pool of shadow. They reached it. MacNab made his turn and the headlamps lit up, for a brief moment, a wide green door into which was set a smaller and narrower door.

'This is it,' the Picaroon said. He reached round behind him, picked up a coil of rope. 'I'll slip out. Lockwood should let himself out at once. That was the idea.'

'Keep your eye on that dog,' the Scot said grimly.

Ludovic tapped his pocket. 'I've got his medicine here, Mac. One little whiff and he'll be out for half an hour and when he does get over it he'll be a sleepy little dog for as long as we need to worry about.' He eased open the car door, stepped out and crossed to the shadow of the big door itself. For a moment he listened. 'Are you there, Lockwood?'

There was no answer.

For a minute or so he waited, but there was no sound from the other side of the wall. The Picaroon came to a quick decision and returned to the car. 'There's no sound at all, Mac. No sign of him. I don't like that.'

'What do you think?'

'He said he would be listening and watching for us and come out as soon as he heard us. So far he's made no movement.'

'Maybe he hasn't heard us.'

'I doubt that. If he was listening he couldn't have failed to hear us. And whether he heard or not, the dog would have heard us.' He thought for a moment. 'We can't wait here for very long. We could be taken too easily. Give me the wire-cutters.'

'What are you going to do?' MacNab handed them over.

'Get over the top of the gate and find out what has happened. Wait here. Give me five minutes. I won't be more than that.' He went back to the gate, looked upwards gauging its height in the dim light, then leapt upwards. His fingers gripped the top of the door and he drew himself upwards. A moment more and he was perched precariously on top of it. He drew the wire-cutters from his pocket, snipped through one or two strands of barbed wire then replaced them. A moment more and he was in the small square yard, staring towards the building.

For a moment he halted there, rigid, listening, his ears alert for any sound, but the premises were silent and he moved towards the building itself. It was squarish and brick-built, and there were two windows facing him with a door on the left. He groped in his pocket for a set of picks, then tried the handle. It turned in his hand and the door opened.

He pushed it inwards, gently, till it touched the wall, stepped inside and produced a small pocket torch. He swung it round, waist high. There was a door on his right, and another door on his left. The door on his left was open and led to the saw mill itself. Even with the wan light of his torch he saw the glint of machinery, and when he sniffed, sensed the aromatic smell of wood.

He walked towards it, swept the torch around. Two circular saws close at hand to him, a little stack of planking and a stronger odour of wood and sawdust.

He stepped backwards and approached the door on his right, tried it gently. It swung open as he turned the handle and he stepped inside swinging the torch around. The beam touched a wall cupboard, a desk with a telephone on it, a chair which had been knocked over and which lay on the floor.

There was a dark, shapeless mass beyond it.

The Picaroon stepped forward very slowly and trained the beam on it.

The man who lay there was perhaps fifty. He lay on his face and there was a little ruby-coloured pool at his head. A thick set, strongly built man. He had been shot at close range. There was a smallish hole above his left eye where the bullet had gone in and a trickle of blood oozing from behind the dead man's right eye.

The Picaroon moved back to the door. He used his handkerchief to wipe the handle with thoroughness, went outside and cleaned the handle of the outer door. He crossed to the gate and leapt upwards with all the skill and grace of a trained gymnast. Very gently he dropped to the roadway on the other side, reached the car and swung open the door. He slid inside, closed the door gently and looked at MacNab.

'Let's get out of here, Mac. Quickly too.'

MacNab's foot moved towards the clutch. 'Where's Lockwood?'

'Dead!' said the Picaroon and for the return journey sat in grim silence.

15

It was one o'clock. The Picaroon, who had made an interesting phone call, and had not gone to bed till after six o'clock, slept until high noon, had breakfasted on bacon and eggs, kidneys and tomatoes, with a more than reasonable lashing of toast and marmalade and was working on his third cup of coffee when MacNab appeared, dressed for the kitchen and filling his pipe.

'Have you had all you're needing? A wee bit more toast, maybe?'

'I'm replete,' Ludovic said. He lit a cigarette. 'Take off your pinny, Mac, and sit down. I want to talk.'

MacNab stripped off the green coarse apron he affected upon these occasions, sat down and struck a match. 'I don't like the look of this business at all, at all.'

'No more do I,' the Picaroon said. 'It could be very unpleasant.'

'Back where we started.'

The Picaroon shook his head. 'Not by a long way, Mac, old boy. We know something now. What's behind it—and who's behind it. The bullion robbery.'

'Usher?'

'Presumably. And Donlevy. Usher may have done a fair amount of the planning and spade work. Donlevy and his crowd were responsible for the job itself.' He thought for a moment. 'If Lockwood was right, he saw Donlevy. That makes you think. If I'd been in his shoes I'd have got out of the country.'

'Maybe he was,' MacNab said, 'and came back.'

The Picaroon looked over at him with interest. 'You know, you could be right about that. I hadn't thought of it that way.' He rose and strode up and down the room. 'Lockwood was certain enough that he'd seen Donlevy and Lockwood knew him. He'd met him in Australia years before.'

'He wouldn't be likely to make a mistake?'

'I doubt it. Lockwood had some experience in security work, and he was a capable sort of fellow. No, he wouldn't be likely to make a mistake. Besides, it wasn't just Donlevy. He mentioned Kuvelik too. Kuvelik was Donlevy's number one.' He looked thoughtful. 'We're going to get Peter in on this one. What we need is a conference. My guess is that we're going to need all the help we can get. We don't know enough about the details of the bullion robbery. That sort of lark is right up Peter's alley. I shouldn't like to—'

There was a sudden, sharp peal and MacNab looked over his shoulder in annoyance. 'What's that but the doorbell at this time of the day? You would wonder who it could be that's got time on his hands for the private visit at one o'clock of the day.' He rose and made his way through the hall.

There was the sound of the front door opening, then the mutter of voices. A moment more the door opened and MacNab ushered in Chief Superintendent Wheat.

'Look who's here!'

The Picaroon stared. 'Septimus? What's the idea? Have they broken you?' There was genuine surprise, almost consternation in his voice. 'Has the revolution arrived?'

'What revolution are you talking about?' Wheat asked coldly.

'Have the masses risen and submerged the aristocracy of brains?'

And, indeed, there was some valid reason for his honest amazement, for, in the old days, Chief Inspector Septimus Wheat had been the arch-opponent of the Picaroon. To his desk at Scotland Yard there came, automatically, every complaint, every fragment of correspondence which dealt with the exploits of the Picaroon. In those days it had been Wheat's chiefest ambition to lay one large white hand on the shoulder of the Picaroon and say:

'Ludovic Saxon, I have here a magistrate's warrant for your arrest on a charge of such-and-such, and I have to warn you that anything you say will be taken down and may be used in evidence. Kindly get your hat and coat.'

It is a matter of history that the words were never delivered. Over the years had come a bond of what was almost affection between the two adversaries. Promotion had come to Septimus Wheat, and he had other fish to fry. When they met now, and it was seldom that they did, it was usually over a convivial pint in a pub which both favoured from time to time and the occasion was one of reminiscence.

'Sit down,' MacNab said, 'and I'll get you some beer.'

Wheat sat down. 'I don't want beer.' He very often said that, but he was usually glad enough to get it.

MacNab disappeared into the small ale department. When he emerged he bore a tall bottle, with the cap removed, and a tumbler. 'Here you are. Take your usual.'

Wheat received it, poured out with a practised hand and swallowed a mouthful. 'Thanks. I was a little dry.'

The Picaroon eyed him curiously. 'What's up, Septimus?'

Wheat looked over the top of his glass at him. 'Behaving yourself these days, Mr. Saxon?'

'Reasonably well.'

'You're trying hard then?'

'He's taking both hands to it,' MacNab said stonily.

'Funny.' Wheat took some more beer. 'Where were you last night be . . .'

The Picaroon shook his head. 'I knew it, Mac. Old Septimus has been demoted or whatever they call it on the force.'

'Disrobed,' MacNab said.

'Disrobed,' Ludovic repeated. 'They've got him back in his old job, Mac, and he's starting in where he left off. "Where were you last night between . . ." '

'That should have been, more properly,' Wheat said placidly, 'between the hours of one o'clock and two-thirty this morning.'

The Picaroon turned round. 'Where was I, Mac?'

'In your bed—and I'll bet Wheat was in his.'

'There you go, Septimus,' the Picaroon said. 'That proves it. Next question.'

Wheat shook his head. 'You were not. Your car was seen in Baron Alley, Camden Town at approximately one-fifty-eight. It was seen by an elderly gentleman by the name of Steinman, and it was drawn up in front of Connelly's Saw Mill which is situated at the closed end of Baron Alley.'

'You've got it all taped,' the Picaroon said admiringly.

'I have. Mr. Steinman lives across the road from Connelly's. He suffers from asthma and when he has a bad bout he often goes through to his front room and sits at the window for an hour or so at a time. He says he can breathe better that way. After a spell of it he can usually get to sleep again.'

'It's a wonder to me he can sleep at all,' said MacNab indignantly.

Wheat shrugged. 'Anyway, he saw the car—a black Jaguar. He didn't make any mistake. He used to work in Pettifor's Garage in Camden Town and he knows a Jaguar when he sees one. He also saw your number and noted it down. Another thing he noted was that the car waited for eight minutes in front of Connelly's premises. During that time, he saw someone leave the car, climb over the gate and disappear. What happened after that, he doesn't know, but he says that you were gone for five minutes by his watch.'

'I was?' Ludovic was interested.

'Someone was,' Wheat commented. 'It could have been MacNab, though I've never seen him climbing an eight-foot wooden door.'

'I could do it easy,' MacNab said.

Wheat sighed. 'We won't argue about it. The climber was gone for five minutes. When he returned, he got into the car and it was driven away. On his watch it left at exactly six minutes past two.' He looked around. 'Any comments?'

Ludovic sighed. 'This ancient gentleman—is he a time-and-motion man by any chance?'

'He's retired and as smart as a whip.'

'Pretty fond of figures, isn't he?'

Septimus Wheat beamed. 'On the subject of figures, a call came through to divisional headquarters at precisely two twenty-one. The caller rang from a public kiosk in Flock Street. He reported that there was a dead body lying in the office premises of Connelly's Saw Mill at Baron Alley, Camden Town.'

'Interesting,' the Picaroon said.

'It was all that,' Wheat agreed. 'What's more it was true. Sergeant Sangster and P.C. Willis of that division paid a call at Connelly's. They found, first of all, the body of a dead Alsatian. It turned out to be a guard dog which had the run of the yard at nights and it had been poisoned.

'Inside the building, they found the body of a dead man, as advised. He had been shot. He has since been identified as Jack Lockwood, a private investigator, and a man who on investigation has been missing for several days.'

The Picaroon sighed. 'Whatever else your promotion has done for you, Septimus, it has improved your approach. You've got all your facts in order.'

'Do you want to say anything?'

'I don't know that I do,' Ludovic said.

Wheat looked towards MacNab. 'Do you?'

'I want to ask something. Do you want any more beer?'

A faint shadow passed over Wheat's pale, flaccid features. 'Never mind beer.'

'He wants it,' Ludovic said. 'You know Septimus well enough by this time, Mac. Give him another bottle.'

'Smart,' MacNab said. He came back wiping the neck of it on a napkin. 'I drew it for you out in the kitchen.' He poured the contents into the tumbler.

Wheat accepted it without comment. When the bottle had been disposed of he said, 'Now I'll tell you something, Mr. Saxon. You visited Connelly's this morning and you put through the alarm call to D.H.Q.' He sat back.

There was a little silence.

'Guessing,' Ludovic said.

'Do you want to make a statement?'

'No. I'd like to ask a question though.'

Wheat inclined his head to indicate that such a course was permissible.

'What's the idea of worrying you with this hurry-up call to woodyards, Septimus—especially to woodyards at Baron Court?'

'Baron Alley,' Wheat corrected. He looked thoughtful. 'It's a good question. It's a better question than perhaps you know.'

'Then that's going to make it even more interesting to answer, Septimus. Correct me if I'm wrong.'

'You're dead right,' Wheat said pleasantly. 'Lockwood's body was taken away. We had a rush job on it. At the p.m. they found the bullet. The forensic fellows checked up on it and sent their report to me at once.'

Ludovic was honestly puzzled. 'You're not on the Murder Squad, Septimus?'

'No—but I'm in charge of the investigation into the big bullion robbery which took place on the Southampton road in . . .'

The Picaroon said softly, 'You are? I wasn't in the country when it happened, Septimus. These details escape one. Brutal business, wasn't it?'

'Two men were shot dead,' Wheat said. 'A third died only six weeks ago—more or less as a result of the wounds he had received.' He waited a moment. 'We got the bullets that killed those two men, Mr. Saxon, and the comparison microscope shows us that Lockwood was killed in the early hours of the morning by a bullet fired from the same gun.'

There was a long silence.

'Queer business,' the Picaroon said.

'So I want information.'

'You don't think that I was mixed up in your bullion steal, Wheat?'

Wheat shook his head. 'It never entered my head that you were.'

'I was in Australia around that time.'

'The crowd who pulled that one were an Australian bunch. Chris Donlevy, a fellow called Kuvelik, Matt Marsden, the Blue Parrot.'

'I've heard of them,' Ludovic said. 'I've read about that job, Wheat. I suppose just about everyone in the kingdom who can read has read about it. According to the story, Donlevy is a very rough character. The gold was never found.'

'It will be,' Wheat said. 'Some day. I can promise you that.'

'Also according to the story, Donlevy got out of the country right away.'

'That was the theory of it '

'So that it looks now as if Donlevy has come back.'

'That's what it looks like.'

'Tough babies these Australians,' Ludovic said. He shook his head. 'I hope you're keeping your hand in with a bit of target practice now and again, Sep. I shouldn't like anything to happen to you.'

'Nothing is going to happen to me,' Wheat told him bluntly.

'Well, I hope you're keeping up your insurances for all that,' MacNab said. 'Now, with these kind of chaps running around loose. It's a wonder to me the police don't do something about it.'

'The police will do something about it,' Wheat said evenly. 'All right, Mr. Saxon, you were at Connelly's last night.'

'I thought it was this morning.'

'This morning, then,' Wheat said. 'You found Lockwood.'

'No.'

'I want to know why you went there.'

The Picaroon shook his head. 'Nothing doing, Wheat. You say I was there. I say I wasn't, and all the evidence you've got is supplied by an old man who sits up at night with dysentery.'

'Asthma.'

'I stand corrected. Asthma. I'm sorry for the poor old man. I'm sorry for you. Most of all I'm sorry for Lockwood. But I can't tell you anything.'

'You put through the call,' Wheat said.

The Picaroon sighed. 'Hark at him, Mac. Wheat's on the rampage again. Who would ever have expected this?'

'That close to the New Year too,' MacNab said with genuine concern.

Wheat eyed them in turn. 'Old Mr. Steinman saw your car. I got that from him this morning when I questioned him. He made a statement to Detective Sergeant Quinn and Quinn took me round to see him.'

'And how was the poor old gentleman?'

'He was definite,' Wheat said coldly. 'Quite definite. He impressed me and he impressed Detective Sergeant Quinn.'

The Picaroon sniffed. 'Anything will impress a divisional detective sergeant, Septimus. You haven't been a policeman all these years without learning that.' He shook his head. 'No, that's it all over for today. No comment.'

Wheat stared at him for a long, long moment, then picked up his hat.

'You haven't finished your beer,' MacNab pointed out.

Wheat looked into his glass, emptied it and laid it down again. He looked at Ludovic with a cold blue eye. 'All right, Mr. Saxon. You've said your piece, now I'll say mine. I'm not satisfied. I'll be back—soon.' He swung round and walked briskly from the room.

MacNab followed him out in silence. A moment later the outside door slammed shut.

16

The Picaroon listened pensively to the solid tread of MacNab's return along the hall. When he came into the sitting-room, Ludovic said, 'Wheat on the job again.'

'And on his dignity.' MacNab shook his head admiringly. 'I never knew he had as much. It just goes to show you.'

Ludovic picked up a cigarette and lit it from the open fire with a twist of paper. 'Old Wheat is nobody's fool. He knows enough to make it very uncomfortable for us, Mac, and my guess is he's in the mood to do it if we don't take charge of matters ourselves.'

'What are you going to do?'

'Get Peter over.' The Picaroon crossed to the phone and put through a call. When he had Peter Saltmarsh, he said, 'Peter, I'd like you to come over here as soon as possible.'

'It isn't very convenient. What's happened?'

'Trouble. I'll tell you when you get here. It's important.'

'I'll be over,' Saltmarsh said. 'I was just going out to lunch. I can skip it.'

'You can get something here. Mac can fix something. See you within the hour then.' He hung up. 'What have we got for lunch, Mac?'

MacNab considered. 'There's a nice ox tongue and a bit of a York ham, rolls, bread and butter and cheese and beer. Peter'll be all right. There's many a man will have further to go and fare worse.'

'I well believe it,' Ludovic said. 'We'd better get things ready for him.'

'Just you leave that to me,' MacNab said. 'I like to cut hams and things by myself. It's a gift you might say, like playing the pipes, and it's not everybody that can do it. I've seen you make a fine hash of it yourself before now. Just you go and read a paper or smoke and leave it to me.' He disappeared into the kitchen.

Peter Saltmarsh appeared little more than half an hour later, pale-faced and shivering slightly, for an east wind had been blowing since early morning and it carried sleet in the teeth of it.

The Picaroon welcomed him briskly. 'Heat yourself at the fire, Peter. I'll give you a drink. Mac has fixed us with a meal. While we're eating I'll tell you what the position is. So far as I can see it's awkward.'

MacNab wheeled in the big trolley and when they had settled the Picaroon made himself a large sandwich, flourished it and leaned back in his chair. He went over the events of the past thirty-six hours, and Saltmarsh nibbled at his own sandwich and listened in silence till the Picaroon had finished. When he had, the little man looked over.

'You've got yourself into something, Ludovic. Huth, Lockwood, attempts on your own lives and now Lockwood himself. It looks as though you're right about the bullion job.'

Ludovic nodded. 'I can't see how I can be wrong. The Australian link is too strong. Huth was an Australian journalist. Donlevy and Kuvelik and the rest of them are Australian. Lockwood himself had been in Australia. It isn't a job I know much about.'

'It was big,' Saltmarsh said, 'and it was brutal. Two

security men were shot dead. Another one died later from injuries he received. Donlevy had a reputation for hardness. He was an ex-policeman himself.'

'So I understand.'

'It must have helped him a bit to know how the opposition would think,' Saltmarsh said. 'Anyway, they made a job of it.'

'Did the police get anyone at all?'

'In fact they did,' Saltmarsh said. 'Cobber Collins. He was one of the drivers, but I don't think he was much use to them. He's on the Moor now.' He looked over at Ludovic. 'It was a clean, well-planned job. Donlevy knew what he was going after and he got it. He could have got out of it more easily if there had been no shooting, but two of the guards came out fighting and Donlevy used the gun. It was a .38—an Army issue.'

'And what happened afterwards?'

'They got clean away. The gold had been carried in two specially constructed vans. They blasted them open on the spot, transferred the gold to their own transport and escaped without being obstructed.'

'That wouldn't be easy,' Ludovic said. 'Handling the gold. It's a pretty heavy commodity, Peter.'

Saltmarsh nodded. 'That was why there were so many of them on the job. All big fellows too. Donlevy, Kuvelik. This chap they called the Blue Parrot. He was a strong man in a circus at one time.' He pushed aside his plate. 'What happens now?'

The Picaroon lit a cigarette. 'We can't wait for things to develop. Not any longer. I could pass what I've got over to Wheat and take a back seat.'

'But you don't want to do that?'

Ludovic sighed. 'How well you know me, Peter. Besides, there's money in it. One must eat to live, and look at the cost of food.' His eyes darkened. 'And there's Huth and Lockwood. I've never walked out on a job yet, just because things looked awkward. I don't propose to do it now.'

'I never imagined you would,' Saltmarsh said quietly, 'but it isn't working out as you expected.'

'It isn't. My own opinion was that Huth had got into something, but I didn't imagine it was anything as heavy as this. I had the idea it would be fairly straightforward. Huth had discovered something. Huth was awkward. Huth was put into a corner some place till the job was done and the danger was over.' He smiled faintly.

'The same applied to Lockwood. Lockwood had gone after Huth. Lockwood had been warned off, maybe chased off. Only it wasn't like that at all.'

'And you know the reason why it wasn't.'

'Three-quarters of a million in gold,' the Picaroon said. 'What do you do with all that gold, Peter?'

'You have to store it. You have to hide it.'

'Where?'

'If I knew that,' Peter Saltmarsh said, 'I wouldn't be sitting here, Ludovic.'

The Picaroon reached for a cigarette. 'Let's think this one out. Donlevy pulled the job, but I don't suppose Donlevy did the thinking. It would be planned by Usher.'

Saltmarsh nodded in silence.

'There wouldn't be much left to chance,' Ludovic said. 'The hiding-place would be arranged in advance. There would be plans to get Donlevy and the rest of them out of the country at once.'

Saltmarsh agreed. 'The popular idea was that they were on the Continent within twenty-four hours of the robbery. That was probably right. It's easy enough to work it, by plane, by motor launch, especially if you can back it up with money and this crowd would have plenty of money.'

'So all they had to do was to sit back and wait for the heat to die down?'

'That's what it amounts to.'

The Picaroon looked thoughtful. 'A steal like this generates an awful lot of heat.'

'And people have short memories,' Peter said. 'A job like this is a seven days' wonder. At the end of that time, unless the law have turned something up, people begin to forget. Three months afterwards the only people who remember are the police and the newspapers and the only reason they remember is because they're working on it.'

'I suppose that's true.'

Saltmarsh shrugged. 'Of course it's true. Think about the Great Train Robbery. The only thing that kept it alive was the activity of the police and the newspapers. People never talked about it. They just weren't interested. Think of the money the last government looted from us over the past few years. Even when it comes out of their own pockets, people still forget, so long as a little more comes filtering in to replace it.'

'Man, but it's a fact,' MacNab said. 'A pound used to be of some consequence. If you put one in your pocket now, by the time you take it out it's lost a shilling or two in value. It's the same the world over.'

Ludovic had risen to his feet. Now he walked up and down the thirty-odd feet of the comfortable room, and his companions watched him. After a moment or so he came back. 'Right, Peter. I want you to check up on Usher's staff.'

'You won't get much there. The police have been trying to do something with him for years now.'

'I'm not the police,' Ludovic said. 'I'd like to learn something. Check on his office staff. This Miss Prosser and the old Italian chap.'

'Carraccini?'

'That's the one.'

Saltmarsh looked at him curiously. 'Have you got something, Ludovic?'

'An idea.' The Picaroon lit a cigarette. 'No more than that.'

'Is it an idea we can hear something about?'

Ludovic considered. 'Not for the moment, old son. I could be a mile off the beam. In fact, I have to be. Nothing could be so ridiculous!' He shook his head as though the fatuous nature of his own opinion appalled him.

Peter Saltmarsh looked at the wall clock and edged back from the table. 'I've got to go now, Ludovic. I'll do what I can on this Donlevy business. All I say, most of it should be on the files. I'll ring you when I've got something.'

'And keep Tempest on the girl.'

'That would be wise,' Saltmarsh said, 'in view of the disappearance of her husband and of the murder of Lockwood.'

MacNab moved to the door. 'I'll get your coat, Peter.' He went through to the cloak-room and returned with the coat draped over his arm. 'Here you are. Fine and warm. I had it sitting on the radiator no less.' He held it for Saltmarsh.

Peter Saltmarsh drew on his leather gloves, and when he had done so, looked at the Picaroon. 'You think that Usher has been behind this bullion job, Ludovic?'

'That's the idea I've formed.'

Saltmarsh shrugged. 'You may be right. It would be tidy-minded to have that idea. Usher could be involved in it. I don't say he isn't, but I can tell you one thing. The police have put a lot of work into this one, and the man they have in mind as the brains behind it all isn't Usher.'

Ludovic stared at him. 'Who is he?'

'Mr. Raphael.'

There was a little silence.

Ludovic said, 'Mr. Raphael? Who is he?'

'Your guess is as good as mine,' Saltmarsh said. 'Anyway, that's the whisper. The police believe it too, I can tell you that. I got that from Inspector Stanton as long as a year past. I haven't heard they've changed their mind. You haven't heard of him?'

'Of Mr. Raphael?' Ludovic shook his head.

'Not many people have,' Saltmarsh admitted.

'We've been out of the country a lot in the past eighteen months.'

'He's been around that long,' Saltmarsh said. 'The story is he planned the big bank robbery at Brisbane four years ago. They took two hundred thousand dollars from the Bank of Western Australia. Used a plane to get away. It was a very well-organised job. The Donlevy crowd worked that one.'

Ludovic was fascinated. 'And Raphael planned it?'

'That's what the police say,' Peter Saltmarsh said. 'They don't know any more about Raphael than I do, mark you. He's just a name. He could be Donlevy himself. He could be Kuvelik. All they know is that he is a master of detail. Nothing goes wrong on his jobs. So goes the whisper.'

'And no one knows anything about this mysterious Mr. Raphael?'

'No. As I say, he could be Donlevy himself. He could be Huth for all I know.'

'And he could be Usher?'

'That's right,' Saltmarsh said. 'Get Wheat to tell you about him next time he comes round. You might get something interesting.' He edged away. 'Now I must get along. I'll keep in touch.'

The Picaroon raised a hand in salute. 'I'll think it over.' He moved towards the telephone.

MacNab said, 'A fine idea. This way, Peter.' He moved ahead towards the door. When he came back, the room was empty, but from the Picaroon's bedroom came the sound of hurried dressing.

17

MacNab was filling his pipe by the fireside when the Picaroon emerged from his bedroom and came through to join him. He wore a suit of his favourite grey, a grey shirt with a narrow tie, and in his eye was a dancing little light MacNab knew of old.

'It's you that looks in form,' he said and Ludovic nodded.

'This thing begins to get interesting, Mac.'

'Where are you off to now?'

'To the *Post Courier*. I want to see Grant. I rang him. He'll give me five minutes. A tough baby this Mr. Grant.'

'He'll be an East Coast man,' MacNab said. 'Them Grants is a hard lot. I could tell you a thing or two about the Grants.'

'Some other time,' said Ludovic. 'I'm on my way. If Wheat comes back, play him gently, Mac. We don't want trouble there.'

'Like a fish,' MacNab agreed. 'You don't need to tell me.'

'I don't think I do.' The Picaroon left and made his way by tube to Blackfriars, and thence to the offices of the *Post Courier*. A commissionaire took his name, made a confidential little phone call, then nodded. 'You know your way up, sir?'

The Picaroon agreed that he did. He made his way towards Grant's room and was ushered in by the editor's capable secretary to where Grant sat at his desk, packing shag into his big-bowled pipe.

He looked up and nodded as the Picaroon appeared. ''Afternoon, Mr. Saxon. Back again. You think you've got something?'

Ludovic, who was a firm believer in preliminaries, sighed. 'You don't waste much time in getting down to business, Mr. Grant.'

Grant smiled a faint and frosty smile. 'Not many people in my line of business do. Time is our ally, but time is also our greatest enemy. We have to make the most of it. We sell and disseminate news. Yesterday's news is as dead as Ur of the Chaldees.'

'It's a point of view,' Ludovic admitted.

'What do you want?'

'I've been looking into this business,' Ludovic said.

'Have you got anywhere?'

'Yes. Farther than I thought.'

There was a sudden glint of interest in Grant's eyes. 'Have you now?'

'There's a story in it.'

'I thought there would be,' Grant said. 'Anything that attracts Huth would be bound to have some news value.' He looked at the Picaroon keenly. 'We ran a column on this Lockwood killing. Has that anything to do with it?'

'Maybe,' Ludovic said thoughtfully. 'But we are not here to talk of Lockwood, Mr. Grant. We are here to talk of Huth.'

'What about him?'

Ludovic said bluntly, 'I want a list made out of how he spent his working hours over the last month. Can you arrange that?'

The editor frowned. 'That's a pretty vague request.'

'It's a very necessary one—and it has to be done quickly.'

'How quickly?'

'It can't be done too quickly,' Ludovic said. 'I've got to have the information and you're the only person who's in a position to provide it.'

Grant picked up a long, yellow pencil and toyed with

it. 'If I thought it was justified I could put a man on to it. Mark you, it might not be complete, because Huth was, to a very large extent, a free-lance. He didn't clock in. He didn't work to the sort of hours that I do, for example. Some days he wasn't here at all. Some nights he appeared when he wasn't expected.' He spread out his hands. 'I could make a stab at it, but it would take time. It would also take a very good man off his usual job. As I say, it would have to be justified.'

'I think it could be.'

'Go ahead and justify it.'

Ludovic said slowly, 'And if I do, for the moment, this is confidential?'

'If you say it has to be—it will be confidential.'

'It has to be.'

'But ultimately there will be a story in it?'

'I'd say a very big one.'

'Tell me.'

Ludovic leaned forward. 'You remember the gold bullion robbery?'

Grant's eyes flickered. 'I remember that. You think Huth's disappearance was linked up with that?'

'I think it was,' the Picaroon said. 'At the moment there's no direct evidence at all, but I've got an idea that it might be possible to find some.'

Grant turned the pencil upside down and put the tip of his finger on the point. He leaned over and flicked a switch. 'Ask Miller to come here at once, please.' He looked across to where the Picaroon sat. 'I'll put Miller on it. Tell him what you want. He's the best man I can think of for a job like this.'

Miller appeared a moment or so later. He was a man of average height, paunchy and with dull, sallow features and iron-grey hair. He wore a yellow shirt with a green necktie which did nothing for his complexion at all, and his dark eyes looked sleepy.

Grant said, 'This is Mr. Saxon, Miller. He's chasing up Larry Huth. Give him all the help you can. He wants a specific job done. He'll tell you about it. Do the best you can and as quickly as you can. That's all.'

Miller nodded. 'Very good, Mr. Grant.' He looked at Ludovic. 'This way, Mr. Saxon.' He led the Picaroon out of the room down a wide stairway and into a large general office. On either side were a number of cubicles and he crossed towards one and ushered the Picaroon within.

There was one chair in it, and a small desk. Miller pushed the chair across. 'Sit down, Mr. Saxon.' He sat on the desk himself, produced a packet of Players and held it out. 'Smoke?'

The Picaroon took one and produced a lighter.

'What is it you want, Mr. Saxon?'

The Picaroon told him.

Miller sat, staring over his head and rubbing his knuckles across his ill-shaven chin. When the Picaroon had finished, he said, 'You want a list of Huth's assignments for a month before he disappeared?'

'A month should cover it. Can it be done?'

'It can be done all right,' Miller said thoughtfully. 'Larry isn't the most regular creature I can think of, but it can be done. Mark you, there could be gaps.'

'I suppose so. How long is it going to take?'

Miller nibbled on a fingernail. 'Hard to say. It's a matter of getting the staff together and asking questions. A fair amount will be listed in the assignments' book, but a lot of things happen that don't get listed there or anywhere else. The biggest job will be to get hold of the reporters.' He looked down irritably at the nail which was troubling him. 'A friend of Larry's?'

'I've never met him.'

'He's got a wife,' Miller said. 'You might get something there. I've met her once or twice. You should talk to her.'

'I might.'

Miller nodded. 'Never know what could come out of it, do you? It's a funny business about Larry. No one can figure it out. There's been a lot of talk about it too.'

'I'll bet,' agreed Ludovic. 'What's the general opinion of his fellow men?'

Miller took the cigarette out of his mouth. 'Two schools. The young ones—or at least some of 'em—think he's gone off with another woman. Anyone who knows him isn't going to buy that. You know how it is though. The young ones always look for a romantic angle. Boy meets girl. They never really get out of that till they get married themselves. That fixes 'em.'

'And then there's a second school as you say.'

'Yes. Those who think like me that Larry poked his nose too deep into something. That can happen more often than you know. A reporter can hear a lot. Especially if he's on crime. Surprise you what you do pick up, and, of course, every now and again somebody hears something he shouldn't which means trouble.'

'You've known it to happen before?'

'Once or twice. You won't get anyone to talk about it though. A man goes adrift for a week or two. Sometimes for a month or two. He turns up in the end, but he's never very willing to talk about where he was or why he went.' He slid from the desk. 'Right, Mr. Saxon. Do what I can.' He leaned over and opened the door. 'Like a bunch of battery hens, aren't we? Who would imagine that the immortal prose you read in your leading articles was written by a fellow cooped up in one of these?'

'When shall I hear from you?'

'Tomorrow,' Miller said. 'Morning, perhaps, if you're lucky. Can you give me a telephone number?'

The Picaroon handed him a card. 'Thank you.'

Miller put it in a waistcoat pocket without looking at it. 'Right, Mr. Saxon. Lift's just through the doorway there. I'd better get down to it.'

The Picaroon agreed and went downstairs to the reception desk.

18

Anne Pennant was checking over a number of green cards, in the drawer of a cabinet. She looked up as he came forward, then looked again. 'Oh, good afternoon, Mr. Saxon. I thought I recognised you.' She pushed the cards aside.

'Done any remembering yet?'

She sighed. 'I'm afraid not. Is it really so important?'

'I think it is. I'd like you to keep on trying.'

'It's not going to work. I have tried. Very hard too.'

Ludovic beamed. 'Keep up the good work. It will come to you one of these days. You'll go to bed with your mind a blank and when you waken up in the morning, you'll say, "Bless my jolly old soul, what am I flogging myself like this for? It was old Franky the nice gentleman was meaning," and you'll phone me at once.'

'I doubt it.'

'I don't,' Ludovic said. 'Got any Australian boys on the list?'

She shook her head. 'Not that I can think of.' She thought for a moment. 'I know a New Zealand boy, though he isn't my boy friend, he's Milly's.'

'Who is Milly?'

'A friend of mine. Milly Tarn. We used to live in the same block of flats.'

'And she has a boy friend from New Zealand?'

'Yes. It isn't so remarkable. She's an Australian herself. She's a member of the Down-Under Club. I've gone to one or two of their hops. That was where I met Rick. Rick Stillwell, the New Zealander.'

'Does she know Larry Huth?'

'I should think so. She's never said so. I haven't seen her so often recently myself though.' She thought for a moment. 'She's rather good fun. She took me to the Down-Under Club once or twice for a meal.'

'What does she do?'

'She's a buyer with one of the fashion houses.'

'And you don't see her often now?'

'No. Her work takes her abroad quite a lot. She isn't in London nearly as much as she used to be.'

'Young?'

She looked at him curiously. 'Around forty, I'd say. Why are you asking?'

Ludovic sighed. 'I'm asking a lot of people a lot of things these days. If she's been at the Down-Under Club she may know Larry Huth. Do you know where she lives?'

'Yes, she has a flat at Rennick Road, in Chelsea—15 Rennick Road, but I doubt if you'll be able to find her there. Quite often I've rung up and she hasn't been at home.'

The Picaroon pondered. 'Probably out with her New Zealander. You know what girls are these days. Nice lad?'

She wrinkled up her nose. 'I shouldn't say so. Too old, if you know what I mean. He must be thirty. He's creaking at the knees and everything.'

'Just ready for the knacker's yard,' Ludovic said. 'I can see what you mean. And where does he hang out, this ancient relic?'

'Rick? I've got no idea. Why do you want to know?'

'I don't know that I do,' he said briskly. 'Forget that I asked you that question, old girl. And now I'll leave you to get on with your normal and lawful duties.' He left and made his way out to the street. He walked to Blackfriars, took a ticket for Earls Court, and when he arrived there, picked up a cab and drove round to Lyman's Hotel, then sought the seclusion of his room on the fourth floor.

For half an hour he worked on his appearance, then locked up, made his way to the hall and crossed towards one of the tall narrow windows. He stood there for a few moments, peering down into the street, but although there were a few cars parked in the near vicinity, and some of them held occupants, it was difficult to believe that any of them might have been interested in his own movements. And yet sinister and mysterious happenings had occurred. He thought of Larry Huth—of Lockwood, and of the bullet which had so nearly missed MacNab, and made his way along to the back stairway which led to the servants' quarters at the rear of the building.

He reached the narrow, tiled passage-way, which led to the back of the hotel, without encountering anyone. The door was locked, but the key was in the lock. He turned it gently, slipped outside and closed the door quietly behind him. A pathway led through the grassed area of the back towards a door in the high brick wall.

He let himself out of this and into the alley and a moment more and he was heading towards the underground station.

The light of day was thickening when he reached Baron Alley and looked down towards the end of it. There was a lorry in front of the big gate, which was open and beyond it a small, white car which looked like a sports model.

He walked down towards the woodyard and when he

reached the wide open gate saw that timber was being carried out for loading. The lorry was reversed into the courtyard and halted, all but blocking the gap. He passed it and noted that the white car was indeed a sports car and as such was hardly likely to be a policeman.

He crossed the road now to the grim, old-fashioned tenement, and made for the end entrance. There were six flats, and each of them had a brass name-plate on the door, but none of them bore the name Steinman.

He made his way out to the street again, trying the second entranceway and this time he was more fortunate, for, on the second floor, he found a plate which read

J. S. STEINMAN

The Picaroon touched the bell.

A moment passed, there was the sound of someone approaching. The door opened and an elderly woman peered out at him.

The Picaroon removed his hat. 'Mrs. Steinman?'

'Yes.'

'I wonder if I could have a word with your husband,' he said. 'It's about the business at Connelly's. I won't take any longer than I can help. He's been very helpful to us, and there are a couple of points I'd like to check.'

She held the door open. 'You'd better come in. Father's in the room. He sits in there a lot. He likes to watch what goes on.' She opened a door. 'Father, it's a gentleman from the police.' She ushered Ludovic in. 'I'll just leave you to get on with it. Don't keep Father too long now. He's had a tiring day of it.'

'I won't,' said Ludovic. He went across to the window where Steinman was sitting. 'Good evening, Mr. Steinman.'

Steinman was a thin old man with a narrow, pinched

face, blue eyes and the very fine textured skin one sees in the very old or the very unwell. He looked up at Ludovic now and nodded. His hair was very silvery and smooth and thin, but when he spoke his voice was strong enough. 'Good evening, officer. Sit down.' He pointed to a chair.

The Picaroon sat down. 'I won't take up much of your time, Mr. Steinman, but there has to be just a little more checking done. I understand you were sitting by your window here for about an hour and a half in the early hours of the morning.'

'Yes. Probably for a little bit longer. I very often come through here at night if I can't sleep. I have trouble with my breathing and I have to sit up. If I stay in bed I keep my wife awake.' He smiled faintly. 'I find it better to come through here. I have this little electric radiator to keep me warm—and a good heavy rug.'

The radiator was glowing from one element.

The Picaroon nodded. 'And I understand you were sitting here when you saw this Jaguar draw up here this morning.'

The old man nodded. 'Yes. I saw it arrive. That was at one fifty-eight. I looked at my watch at the time, because I thought it was a very odd time to see a car drive up to Connelly's. When I saw someone get out and climb over, I was pretty certain I was watching burglars at work, though what they would get in Connelly's, I couldn't think.' He looked over at Ludovic. 'The car was there for eight minutes. I timed it. I did think I might have raised an alarm, but it didn't seem worth while. It meant I should have had to waken my wife and have her waken a neighbour.'

'That wouldn't have been very convenient.'

'No—and the nearest telephone is in Pender Street. I thought it better just to say nothing. Besides, you don't know what sort of thing might happen to you these days if you interfere in a thing like that. But of course when the police came questioning everyone about a murder, well, I had to tell them.'

'You did indeed,' Ludovic said. 'We've got all that covered pretty well, Mr. Steinman. What I'm interested in is what happened before the Jaguar appeared.'

Steinman looked over at him. 'I can't tell you that, officer.'

'You mean you'd just come through here?'

The old man pondered. 'I'd been sitting for about ten minutes perhaps, when the Jaguar came. It wasn't any longer than that.'

'That would make it around one forty-eight when you came through.'

'Yes. Say one forty-five,' Steinman said.

The Picaroon looked thoughtful. 'And you didn't see anyone come or go?'

Steinman had seen no movement at all, nor had he heard anything. 'The superintendent says that this dead man had been shot. Maybe so, but I didn't hear a shot. That's all I can say. I did near a car close at hand, but that was later.'

'How much later?'

'About ten minutes later. At two-fifteen. I looked at my watch then too. I didn't see it, but I heard it come in, but it must have turned at once. In fact I know it did. I heard a door open and close and then it drew away.'

'As though someone had got into it?'

The old man nodded. 'That was what I thought myself. That someone had got into it.'

Ludovic pondered. 'Is there another entrance to Connelly's?'

'Yes, there is. On the other side at the back of the tenement.'

'That's all I want to know,' said the Picaroon with satisfaction. He thanked the old man and took his leave. In the hall, he gave the old lady a note, pressing it into her hand. 'Get the old gent a drink with that, Mrs. Stein-man.'

'I'm sure it's very kind of you, sir, but . . .'

He pressed her fingers over it. 'What is Mr. Steinman's hearing like?'

'It's not so good,' she said, 'though he won't admit it, sir. Was he able to help you? I hope he was.'

'He told me something that was very interesting,' the Picaroon said. He thanked her and took his leave.

It was dark now and he made his way thoughtfully along the narrow and ill-lit street. Steinman had indeed given him something which was interesting in the ex-treme, for if his times were right, and they were very likely to be, the arrival of the second car and its speedy departure was very easily understood.

Jack Lockwood's killer must still have been on the premises when he himself had arrived, found the body and left!

He crossed the road now. The tall brick wall that sur-rounded the saw mill ended against the gable of the tenement. The Picaroon went into the first entranceway, walked through to the area at the back and in front of him he saw a continuation of the brick wall. He walked over to it and saw the small door built into it.

He tried the handle and though it was locked, the handle turned easily enough. Satisfied now, the Picaroon walked through the passage-way and into Baron Alley. This then, was how Lockwood had met his death.

The killer had been familiar with Connelly's and must certainly have known of the presence of the guard dog. He must have walked down towards the main gate, then, when he had attracted the dog's attention, thrown over a cyanide capsule in a ball of minced meat. After that, he had come to this side door and had let himself into Con-nelly's, found Lockwood and shot him. He must still have been on the premises when the Picaroon himself had arrived and had waited until he had heard him withdraw before he had taken his own departure.

He walked smartly along to the end of the street and had gone no more than a hundred yards when he saw the telephone kiosk he had already marked down. He stepped into it, glancing down at his watch.

It was five fifty-five. Now he settled himself comfortably and lit a cigarette. He smoked with one eye on the minute hand of his watch, and when it had moved round to six o'clock, he dialled his number and listened to the sound of the alarm at the other end.

For a moment or so he heard it, then came the sound of the receiver being lifted.

'Smail and Usher.' It was Miss Prosser who spoke.

The Picaroon said, 'Dyson here, miss. You met me last night. Mr. Usher said I was to call him at six o'clock tonight.'

'He's in his room, Mr. Dyson. I'll put you through to him.' A moment more and he heard the lawyer's voice.

'Simon Usher here.'

'You told me to ring you up tonight, Mr. Usher.'

There was a little silence.

'Did you put through a call to Joe Prideaux?'

'I did,' Simon Usher said. 'It was satisfactory—up to a point.'

The Picaroon waited.

'There could be something for you,' Simon Usher said at length. 'Subject to certain—ah—investigations being made. These matters are of no concern of mine. However, I have mentioned your name to a client. He may be able to do something for you. Where are you living at the moment?'

'Nothing doing,' the Picaroon said. 'I've been too long at this game to stick my neck out, Mr. Usher. You want to investigate me. Fair enough, but that lark cuts both ways. I have to know where I'm going too.'

There was a second silence.

'Possibly so.' There was a grudging appreciation in

Simon Usher's cold voice. 'That is a matter you will require to take up with this client I have mentioned to you. That is all I can do. All I am prepared to do.' He cleared his throat.

'You will see this person tomorrow night at ten o'clock.'

'Where do I see him?'

'At his office,' Simon Usher said. 'It is situate at 111 Prior Lane. The name of the firm is Becker and Knightly. You will see Mr. Becker. You understand?'

'Yeah,' Ludovic said. 'Mr. Becker of Becker and Knightly at 111 Prior Lane. The time is ten o'clock tomorrow night.'

'That is correct,' said Simon Usher and hung up. For a moment or so he sat in silence at his desk, then he crossed to the door and, opening it, passed along to the general office. He looked into it, but it was empty and the door of the closet in which Miss Prosser hung her coat stood half open.

He went back to his room, closed the door and returned to his desk and reached for the telephone. His long thin forefingers poked at the dial, and after a moment a voice said in his ear :

'Becker and Knightly.'

'Simon Usher speaking. This man Dyson will be calling on you at ten o'clock tomorrow night. You will hear very shortly how you have to deal with him.'

'Very good, Mr. Usher. You can rely on me. I'm not worried about a fellow like that and . . .' Harry Becker realised very suddenly that, although he had not heard the click of the receiver as it was returned to the cradle, he was talking to a dead line and that Simon Usher had hung up.

He licked his dry lips and sat staring at his own receiver. After a moment or so he laid it down.

19

The Picaroon smoked a second cigarette without leaving the kiosk. When he had finished it, he had made his mind up. Now he rang the flat in Courtfield Mews and when MacNab lifted the receiver, 'I'm going to need you to-night, Mac.'

'What's up?'

'Listen,' Ludovic said, and explained.

'I don't like the sound of it,' MacNab said. 'It looks to me like they're sending you along to Becker's to be dealt with.'

'I think you're right,' Ludovic said.

'So you will not go near Becker's place in Prior Lane,' MacNab said firmly. 'Not tomorrow night or any other night. You will just have a nice quiet night by your own fireside and maybe a wee dram to keep your spirits in order.'

'No,' the Picaroon said, 'I think we'll look into it, Mac.'

'What do you mean?'

Ludovic said, 'I think you're right about Usher. I don't think he knows who I am. But I do think he's cagey. My own idea was to edge myself in as a useful man in a pinch. I didn't think he would wear it, but I hoped he would. It could have been a short cut.'

'Did he speak to Joe Prideaux?'

'He says he did. I'm not certain. What I am sure enough about is that he's come to the conclusion that there's no point in taking a chance.'

'And he's right,' MacNab said. 'I couldn't put it better myself. You will just come home and . . .'

'No, I'll play it out,' Ludovic said. 'I'll tell you why. He's sent me to Becker's, as I say—but nothing is going to happen to me at Becker's. He needs Becker. What will happen is that Harry boy will send me some place else for disposal.'

'I see what you mean.'

The Picaroon laughed softly. 'I'm glad you do, Mac. My idea is that if Usher wants to take care of me, he's likely to use the man who took care of Lockwood. That means a confrontation and it's the only way I can see us getting one.'

MacNab thought it over. 'Man, but there could be something in it.'

'I think there is,' Ludovic said. 'We'll talk about it later.'

'You're coming back now?'

'No. I've got a little job to attend to first. Expect me later.' He hung up, walked along to the underground station and returned to Lyman's Hotel. Here he went into the quiet, almost desolate dining-room and had an excellent meal. He smoked a cigarette over it, made his way up to his room on the fourth floor and changed into the more orthodox clothing of his normal life. When he left, it was by the front door, and a cab was summoned to take him to Earls Court station.

He took a ticket here for Sloane Square and when he reached his destination, walked round to Rennick Road. Number 15 was one of a block of tall, old-fashioned houses which had been converted into flats and Ludovic, an authority on such establishments, made a brisk survey.

There was no porter's box at the entrance, but to the left of the stairway, there was a door which led to the rear portion of the house. He eased the door open very gently and as he did so, he heard the sound of coal being shovelled in the basement.

He closed the door silently and walked over towards the stairway. There was a letter rack fixed to the wall here. In it was a series of little pigeon-holes and in some of them, reposed letters. Above each was a small, type-written card and he read them over.

A. J. SYLVESTER. ANTON LAUZON. MISS C. C. KELL.
J. V. SMITH. D. D. VENNING. MISS M. TARN.

There were two letters in Miss Tarn's box.

The Picaroon removed them both and made his way upstairs, treading quietly and with infinite caution. He found Miss Tarn's flat, located on the second floor, and with a small metal slot on the door in which a white card indicated the name of the occupant in black type.

Ludovic put his finger on the bell, pressed it once or twice.

There was no answer.

He tried again. When there was still no answer, he pushed open the flap of the letter box and peered inside.

There was no sign of light at all.

He produced a little set of picks and went to work. Two minutes later he was pushing open the door of the flat. For a second or two he listened, then stepped inside, closing the door behind him. There was a switch at his hand, but he ignored this and drew an electric torch from his pocket, then moved through the flat in a speedy tour of reconnaissance.

There was a kitchenette, bathroom, two bedrooms, and a sitting-room. One of the bedrooms appeared to have been in use recently, for, on the glass-topped dressing-table, he found a faint trace of powder. He returned to the kitchenette and inspected the small fridge.

It held four eggs, a carton of cream, a lemon, a small dish in which were two lamb chops. Beside it, in a green container were diced carrots and green peas. There was also a half-bottle of sauterne, as yet unopened.

He closed the refrigerator and went through to the bedroom. There was a small wardrobe built into one wall. Now he examined this, and if small, it was tightly packed with a selection of frocks, evening dresses, suits, cocktail dresses. It was very evident that Miss Tarn's post as a buyer was a lucrative one.

He went into the sitting-room. It was small, but comfortably and expensively furnished. He drew the blinds, then the heavy velvet shades, and switched on a table lamp. There was a desk in the far corner of the room.

He crossed to it, sat down and examined the letters he had brought up with him.

The first of these was probably a bill. On the upper left-hand corner was printed in red type: KALEY & MANSON, Fabrics. It had been posted in London, S.W.9.

He laid it aside and considered the second.

This was a plain, court style envelope and had been posted in Melbourne. On the upper left-hand corner, a sticker had been placed which read AIR MAIL.

The Picaroon pondered for a moment, then returned it to his pocket for examination at a more propitious moment. Now he concentrated on the desk.

There was a wide but shallow top drawer and, on either side of the knee-hole, two drawers. The wide drawer at the top was unlocked. He drew it open and inspected its contents with a curious eye.

A large sheet of blotting paper, a packet of paper clips, a patent stapler and a round ruler such as bank clerks frequently use. There was also a small sponge, a tin box which held some fragments of sealing wax and some pins.

He closed the drawer and gave his attention to the others. Three of them were unlocked, one was completely empty, another held only a writing pad and two sizes of envelopes, and the third a telephone directory, a dictionary and a little parcel of road maps, tied together with tape.

Ludovic turned now to the fourth drawer and went to work with his 'picks'. Within two minutes it was open and here he found an ancient leather writing-case, ink-spattered and soft with use. He drew it out, laying it on the flat of the desk in front of him, then opened it out.

There was a sheet of much-used blotting paper, curled and worn around the edges. There was fresh stationery of a pale blue colour, with envelopes to match, a number of stamps of varying denominations, and, in a separate compartment, three larger, manilla envelopes.

He examined the first. It had been posted in Plymouth and the type-written letters from MARKS & MERTON, Estate Agents. The Picaroon read it through pensively. It concerned itself with the remarkable advantages of a 'property of character and distinction which has been in the same family for over eighty years'. It was, the Picaroon noted, 'desirable and offered at a remarkably low price, because the present proprietors are going abroad'. It had, Ludovic noted, been written some two years ago. He returned it to its envelope wondering if Marks & Merton, together with the emigrating proprietor, had managed to get it off their hands as yet.

The second envelope contained no more than correspondence with a firm of motor mechanics over the servicing of a Morris brake.

He turned to the third. It contained half a dozen letters, most of it business correspondence of a heterogeneous variety. A letter from a firm of cabinet-makers discussing the defects of a cabinet which had been sold to Miss Tarn. Another from a travel bureau mentioning the delights of Cyprus; one from the General Post Office concerning a missing parcel, and one from the secretary of the Down-Under Club, enclosing two tickets for a dinner and dance for a date almost two years ago. The tickets had neither been used nor returned. Ludovic wondered if Miss Tarn had paid for them. He was returning them to the envelope when he saw the little scrap of paper which had slid to the floor.

He bent down now to retrieve it, and recognised it as

a clipping from a newspaper. He stared at it with fascinated eyes.

FOR SALE. Quiet country house less than two hours by road from London. The Pines, Hillmeet, Berks. This desirable family residence consisting of . . .

'Well! Well!' said the Picaroon. 'That such things should be!' He read it over twice, returned it to the envelope from which it had fallen, replaced the envelope in the letter-case, deposited the case where he had found it and re-locked the drawer.

He switched off the light, drew back the curtain and pulled up the blinds, then made his way towards the door and stood there listening for a moment.

There was no sound at all.

He let himself out into the narrow hall, walked silently downstairs and returned the letter from Kaley & Manson to the pigeon-hole. The other he retained.

Ten seconds later, he was in the street.

20

The Picaroon arrived at the flat in Courtfield Mews along with a flurry of sleet and MacNab, who had been smoking by the fire, rose briskly to his feet. 'It's yourself, is it? Just you sit down and get your slippers on and I'll see what I can do about a dram for it's the very night for a good one.'

The Picaroon accepted the glass and stuck out his feet towards the fire.

'The best spot on the farm,' MacNab said, 'I'll assure you of that. Listen to that wind and sleet. Did you ever hear the like? It's you and me that's well out of it.'

'But not for long.'

The Scot looked over at him. 'You don't tell me you're going out again in the likes of this? Man, it would be the death of you.'

'We're both going out,' Ludovic said, and proceeded to make the situation clear.

MacNab listened without enthusiasm. 'You want to go at this hour of the night to Hillmeet to prowl through that big house! I'm surprised at you. On a night like this too! What's the matter with tomorrow? The house is not going to go away on you.'

'Tonight's better,' Ludovic said, and told him why.

MacNab was probably convinced. 'If you say so, you say so. It wouldn't be my idea of a job for a winter's night and it coming on for the New Year now. When do you want to leave?'

'Give us an hour yet.' The Picaroon looked at the clock. 'An hour should do us nicely. We'll have to make one or two arrangements.'

MacNab refilled his pipe. 'What's on your mind anyway?'

The Picaroon said softly, 'I paid a visit tonight, Mac, to the Chelsea flat of Miss Millicent Tarn.'

'And who is she?'

'You remember me telling you about Anne Pennant?'

'That's the young lady at the *Post Courier* office?'

'That's the one. Miss Tarn is a friend of hers. They used to live in the same block of flats at one time. They were fairly friendly. She's an Australian and she has a friend who is a New Zealander. His name is Stillwell, Rick Stillwell.'

MacNab's heavy eyebrows twitched. 'An Australian,

is she? There's an awful lot of them going about these days.'

Ludovic said, 'I had a look around her flat. Among other things I discovered that she was interested in country property around Hampshire a couple of years back. In the end, I got the idea she settled for one in Berkshire.'

'What makes you think so?'

'I found a clipping advertising the Pines. I recognised it at once. I remember seeing it in an old newspaper out in Melbourne.' He went on to particularise and MacNab listened, interested.

'Do you tell me that?'

'I do. It looks to me, Mac, as though we are now moving on to the straight run in.' He took the purloined letter from his pocket, looked at it and examined the stamps. 'I'll have a look at this while I'm in the mood for it. Put on a kettle, Mac. We can do with a little steam.'

'You'll get yourself on to bother yet, pinching letters,' MacNab said grimly. 'It's not the thing at all. The postmen are doing it every now and again and you can see for yourself the magistrates take a poor, poor view of it.' But for all that he led the way through to the kitchen, put water into the electric kettle and touched the switch. 'How are we not opening it with a knife?'

'I'll do it this way,' said the Picaroon virtuously. 'The letter may be completely innocent and if it is I'll send it back to her. All you have to do is re-post it and get a stump of pencil and write "Try Chelsea" on it.'

The kettle began to make unhappy, moaning sounds.

Ludovic examined the postage stamps. 'Three of them. It should be simple enough, Mac.' He held them to the spout, steamed them and peeled them off, then returned to the sitting-room. With a small scalpel he made an oblique cut in the envelope in the upper right hand corner which the stamps had covered. From a drawer, he took a small pair of fine forceps, slid them through the cut into the envelope and gripped the single sheet it contained, firmly. He turned it round and continued to do so until the letter itself had twisted itself tightly round the forceps. Now he enlarged the cut and drew it out.

There was but one sheet, and he read it over.

31, Southend Park Street

Sydney.

November 9th.

Dear Milly,

I had a word with Outridge a couple of days ago. I met him by accident, but it was a good job I did. He tells me he was in Adelaide a couple of weeks ago and he heard then that Gordon Wedderburn was making one or two inquiries about you and Chris. You might not know Wedderburn, but he is on the staff of the Adelaide Star, *and it looks like he was making these inquiries for Larry Huth who used to be with the* Star *and is now in London, England. Maybe you have met Huth there. Anyway, I thought you should know. Reporters with long noses can mean trouble.*

All well here. Julie and I are making for New York maybe in the spring. We could see you then.

Best of luck,

Your affct. brother

Harvey.

The Picaroon read it over twice, exultation in his eyes. 'We'll keep it, Mac. I think we can use it.' He handed the letter to MacNab.

The big man produced his spectacles and read it through. When he had done so, he looked at Ludovic over the top of his spectacles. 'This is from her brother?'

'Yes. You'll notice he mentions Chris. I take it he means Chris Donlevy and you know who Donlevy is.'

'It ties it up nicely,' MacNab said. He removed his glasses. 'And where do we find the young lady?'

'We'll get round to that,' Ludovic said. He reached for a cigarette, lit it and blew out a plume of smoke. 'It's working out, Mac. It's working out even better than I expected. I think we're getting somewhere.'

MacNab waited.

'I was wrong about the way I handled it,' Ludovic said. 'Dyson was a mistake, but we all make them. As I told you, I thought there was a chance we might have got into it from their side. It was worth a gamble.' He thought for a moment. 'I don't know yet that they do suspect Dyson. What I do feel is that they could still use him, but if they do, they'll want to put him through it first.'

'Question him?'

Ludovic nodded. 'I think so. This is big-time stuff, and they're big-time operators. They're not going to take Dyson in without a bit more investigation.' He stared at MacNab. 'So the position is they could maybe use Dyson. Whether or not, they want to deal with him. That's why the job was handed over to Becker.'

MacNab nodded in silence.

Ludovic spread out his hands. 'So there it is. On the one hand, they may have decided to put Dyson down, just to be on the safe side. But before they do, they'll want to ask all the questions they can think of before they do anything.'

'On the other, they may be prepared to accept Dyson, question him and fit him into the proper slot. Men like Dyson aren't too easy to come by, so long as they're satisfied he's what he appears to be.' He beamed at Mac-Nab. 'In either event, we're going to have a confrontation—and my guess is that the confrontation will be with Donlevy—with Kuvelik—and possibly with this mysterious Mr. Raphael we've been hearing about.'

'I don't like the sound of it,' MacNab said.

'It's what we've been working for,' Ludovic said cheerfully. 'There are wheels within wheels, Mac.' He changed the subject abruptly. 'I saw Steinman.'

'What did he say?'

The Picaroon told him.

'So the man who killed Lockwood was on the premises when you were there yourself? It's a wonder to me you didn't get it then.'

'It's a wonder to me too,' Ludovic said. 'My guess is he couldn't take a chance with it. His own car hadn't come back for him. He probably thought it had arrived when he heard us drive up. When I came into the building he had to lie quiet. Don't forget the only light was the torch I carried. He wasn't in any position to start a feud in the darkness. What he did was wait for me clearing out, then he slipped out by the back entrance himself, got into the car Steinman heard and scarpered. He couldn't have missed the police by much.'

There was a long silence.

MacNab thought it over. 'I wouldn't say but you're right.'

'I think I am,' Ludovic said. 'Any sign of Wheat?'

'I haven't seen hide or hair of him.'

'You will,' Ludovic said. 'Get in more beer.' He looked at the clock. 'Half an hour more, Mac, and we'll leave.'

'For Hillmeet?'

'For Hillmeet,' said the Picaroon, and rose to make the necessary preparations.

21

The Picaroon was one of those fortunate individuals who could sleep just by putting his head down and closing his eyes. He slept for an hour and a half and it was the touch of MacNab's hand on his arm that wakened him.

'We're just outside the village,' MacNab said. 'Two-twenty and all's well. You know where about this place is better than I do, so you'd better do the driving.'

The Picaroon opened the door silently and stepped out into a cold restless sleet which was whipping about in the thin air. When he had exchanged places with Mac-Nab, he said, 'The thing is fairly straightforward, Mac. We'll drive along to the road that leads up to the Pines. There's a spruce wood on one side of it and scrub on the other. We'll leave the car at a point about half a mile from the house. They've been taking in timber there and there's a road into the wood which will be safe enough because it's had metal thrown on it to take heavy lorries.'

'And after that?'

'After that we walk,' Ludovic said. 'They may have someone on guard. I'd be very surprised if they didn't. We don't want him to hear the car approach.' He stretched out his foot towards the clutch and when they were on their way, 'This should be fairly straightforward. I can't see any great difficulty at all.'

'What about dogs?'

'There may be,' Ludovic admitted. He tapped his pocket. 'I've got enough here to fix them.' He slowed down a little. 'Here's the road.' He swung into it slowly, cut the lights and drove on. After a few moments he peered forward into the darkness. 'There's the cut into the wood.' He slid over it gently and pulled up under the overhang of an oak, switched off the ignition and sat back.

MacNab peered around him. 'As black as the Earl of Mansfield's waistcoat.'

'It won't be so dark when we get out of the wood.' Ludovic leaned backwards, gay and relaxed. 'Right, Mac. I've been in this place before and I don't really expect it to be particularly difficult. We'll go up there together. There's a cloak-room to the left of the front door. In my recollection it presents no difficulties unless these gentry have done some messing about with it. I'll try there. If I get in, I'll open a door so that I can get out in a hurry if need be.'

'A window perhaps?'

'They could be fitted with alarms.'

'Just you watch yourself,' MacNab said. 'Where will I be?'

'There's a stone wall that comes up about to the gable of the house and beyond it is the vegetable garden. In the corner nearest to the house there were one or two holly bushes, if they haven't cut them down. We'll go in there and that's where you'll wait.' He patted his pocket, 'I've got a whistle here. If I have to use it, I will and you're bound to hear it. I've got a gun, which I don't expect to use.'

'It's a useful article the gun,' MacNab said. 'Just you keep it fine and handy. There's no saying the kind of reception you're likely to get.'

The Picaroon opened the door and stepped out of the car, looking at it behind him. He came round to where MacNab was standing, closed the door and locked it. He wore a black ski suit, a black woollen hat, and in the darkness all that could be seen was the lighter patch which was his face. 'We'll go up quietly. A few minutes will take us there. It's no more than four or five hundred yards. We don't want to talk once we get near the house. Anything you want to say now?'

'How long do I give you?'

'Half an hour. That's long enough. In any event, play to the whistle.'

'And if you over-run your time?'

'I'm not likely to, but you could close in. If I can manage it, I'll come out by the way I go in.' He patted his pockets. 'Right. We'll move along.' He stepped out into the shadowed darkness of the wood and they made their way towards the house in silence.

A few minutes brought them to the wall which surrounded it. The Picaroon led the way towards a spot where it passed close to the trees, halted for a moment, then, reaching upwards, drew himself on to the top of it. He remained there in silence, listening, then reached down. 'Right, Mac.'

MacNab pulled his immense weight upwards, threw a leg across the top of the wall, and dropped down to the grass on the other side where Ludovic was already standing.

The Picaroon headed towards the rear of the house, and they passed through a clump of trees. Here he halted for a moment, then: 'There's a light in the window on the gable. I've got an idea that's the main hall. Probably keep it on all night. It can't be on the ground floor. Must be on the first floor. Right, we'll move along. The wall to the vegetable garden is ahead of that. We have to get over that, but it's simple enough.'

'Not a whisper of a dog,' MacNab said hoarsely.

'It's just as well.' The Picaroon moved off. When he reached the wall surrounding the vegetable garden he negotiated it with ease then, when MacNab joined him, pointed ahead and to his left. 'There's the corner I mentioned.'

Two minutes later they were crouched in it, within ten or twelve feet of the house itself.

The Picaroon inspected his watch. 'I'll move off now,

Mac.' He slid away like some shadow of the night and MacNab had no knowledge of his going.

The gable lay in black shadow. The Picaroon merged into it, made his way to the front of the house and located the window in which he had first shown interest. He produced a pen-torch and examined the fittings with scrupulous care.

There was no alarm. He produced a little steel tool, and went to work. Three minutes later, the catch had been forced back. He waited a second or two, alert for any sound, but there was only silence. Very carefully, he edged the lower half of the casement upwards. It slid easily and silently. Ludovic moved his hands on the broad stone sill and leapt upwards.

A second more and he was in the room.

He swung his torch round him carefully. The cloakroom was in full use. On the hooks and hangers were four anoraks, three heavy raincoats, three navy dufflecoats. Cautiously he tried the door.

It was open and he passed out into the hall. He halted here for a moment. His night vision was excellent and after a moment the memory of his previous visit to the house returned to him. He moved along quietly towards the study, aided by the faint glow which reached him from the light on the landing at the head of the stairway.

He tried the door gently. It opened to his touch. The air was warm and comfortable and in the darkness of the room he saw a faint red shimmer from the open fireplace. He stepped inside, produced a larger torch and swung it round.

The room was much as he had remembered it, although the furnishings were different. Now there was a long sofa and four wide armchairs with soiled loosecovers on them. The room reeked of tobacco smoke and when he turned the beam on the hearth he saw several cigarette ends and one or two cigar butts. On a small table was a bottle of Teacher's with no more than an an inch of whisky at the bottom of it.

A longish desk with a telephone on it stood at the window end of the room, and to the right of it a tall and ugly cabinet. Behind it were one or two squares of light which, when he raised the beam of the torch turned out to be pictures.

He left the room, made for the dining-room. It was plainly furnished. Bare boards on the floor, an ancient rug beneath the table and four chairs drawn into place. There was a deal table to act as a serving-table, and on it a wooden tray filled with cheap-looking cutlery. Obviously the house had been furnished with only the scantiest of minimum requirements.

He moved along the hall, opened one door. Inside the room was completely unfurnished. The second door he tried was locked. Now he made his way towards the kitchen premises, pushed open the door of the kitchen itself. There was a warm glow from an oil-fired stove. When he used the torch he saw that on a small blue table were four cups without saucers. To the right of this was a grubby wooden tray with basket-work sides to it, and these were encrusted with grime and fragments of food. On it was a single, large, green plate. It was unwashed and the remains of some sliced meat were pushed to one side of it, as was a crust of bread. Beside it was a large coarse mug and a spoon which had been used to stir some dark substance.

The Picaroon sniffed and thought it had been coffee of a sort. 'Bit of a while since there has been a woman's hand around the place,' he told himself softly. He backed out of the kitchen, stood in the corridor for a moment, listening, but the house was still.

To the left of him was the door that led to the cellar. He tried it, but it was locked. He was about to turn away when he saw that the key, on a length of soiled string, hung on a hook at his hand. He lifted it down, fitted it into the lock and turned.

The door opened.

The Picaroon halted for a moment, dropped the key into his pocket, then, with the beam of light playing on the steps ahead of him, descended into the cellar.

There were ten steps and they led him to a corridor which ran only for the width of the house. To his right was a room without a doorway, but which was built up with wooden racks. There was a smell of must and decay about it, and a pile of sand on the floor gave him the clue he required. This was the vegetable store-room.

He stepped back into the passage, then halted at the next door. It was of solid, heavy wood, and there was no keyhole. Instead, fastened to it was a heavy metal hasp and this was secured by a large, strong padlock the splintered wood around it showing that it had been but recently fitted.

The Picaroon tapped it very gently with his finger-tips. It was even more solid than he had imagined. He placed one ear as close to the edge of the door as was possible and was certain that he heard heavy breathing from within.

Was this the cell which Larry Huth had been confined?

For a second or so he hesitated. He would dearly have liked to make certain, but to do so would have been dangerous. He glanced at his watch. Time was running out for him. Now he went back up the stairway, let himself into the corridor, then locked the cellar door. He replaced the key and moved softly towards the cloak-room. He had all but reached it when he remembered something and made his way back to the study. He slipped inside, crossed towards the tall cabinet and reached up towards the rim of it, ran his fingers around it then withdrew.

A moment more and he was in the hall. He was returning towards the cloakroom when he heard the sound of a door open on the floor above. In a second he had moved into the darkness and stood by the nearly closed door.

Footsteps moved along the hall. He waited a moment then heard the sound of them descending the stairs. A second or two later, someone shuffled through the hall towards the kitchen. The switch clicked on and the light was reflected from the opposite wall along the passage-way.

There was the sound of a kettle being moved across the surface of the stove. Ludovic waited to hear no more. Obviously one of the men tenants had reason to make himself some hot milk or tea. He closed the door of the cloak-room, inspected the window catch and let himself out. He drew down the window and inserted the blade between the sashes. It took no more than half a minute to slide the catch forward. He tried the window, turned back into the shadow.

MacNab was in the corner of the bushes where he had left him. The big man watched him approach, then stretched his limbs cautiously.

'Right,' said the Picaroon and led the way. It was not until they were in the car that he spoke again, and, when he did, he said, 'It worked like a charm, Mac.'

'There was a light went on in one of the upstairs windows. Someone must have heard you. It gave me something to think about, I can tell you.'

'Fellow coming down for his Horlicks,' Ludovic said. 'I heard him.' He touched the starter and in a moment or so they edged forward. He drove slowly and carefully until they had reached the main road and then trod a little more firmly on the accelerator. After a mile or so, he said, 'It could be the end of the road, Mac. They've got someone locked in a room in the cellar.'

'Huth?'

'That's my guess too. I had a notion to prove it, but

it wasn't too safe. I couldn't have got in to him without a screwdriver—and if it had been someone else, the fat would have been in the fire. We'll be back soon though.'

'It's a fact,' MacNab said. 'He's been there for the best part of a fortnight now. He won't go wrong for another day or so.'

'It's the truth, Mac,' Ludovic said. He touched the accelerator and the big car leapt forward into the night. 'Get yourself some sleep. I'll take her back. I'm in the mood for it.'

'Whatever you say yourself,' MacNab said comfortably. 'A bit of sleep never does any harm. I've got a nice wee flask here with what you call the nightcap in it. Will you have a small sensation.'

'Not for me.'

'You know best yourself,' MacNab said. He put the flask to his lips and there was a convivial gurgle. He replaced the stopper and returned the flask to his pocket. 'It's a fine way to start the day,' he said. 'And to end it, too.' He put his head back and a minute or so later he was asleep.

22

The Picaroon slept till noon next morning, shaved, had a tub and ate for two. He was finishing his last slice of toast when MacNab came through, filling his pipe, and dropped into his usual armchair, scanning the table which had been drawn up to the fire with approval.

'I see you took your usual.'

'And enjoyed it, Mac. Some day you'll make somebody a good wife. I've never met anybody yet who could cook the staples of life like you. And when I talk about the staples of life, I am naturally referring to ham, pork sausages, lamb chops, mushrooms, tomatoes and such appetising items.'

'It's a gift,' MacNab said modestly. 'You're born with it or you haven't got it at all. It's not a thing you can learn out of books, though there's any amount of them about. Cookery books, they call them. I wouldn't have one in my kitchen.' He puffed complacently.

The telephone rang as he spoke.

Ludovic moved across towards it, lifting the receiver as he did so. 'Ludovic Saxon.'

A dry voice said in his ear, 'Miller here. *Post Courier*. We met yesterday.'

'Good man,' said the Picaroon. 'Have you got something for me?'

'I've got a list of sorts,' Miller said. 'It isn't very full, but as far as I can see I could have it for a month without being able to add to it. I thought I'd better let you have it if it was to be of any use at all.'

'I'll be glad to have it,' the Picaroon said. 'Shall I call for it?'

'It's on the way,' Miller said. 'Grant told me to send a man in a car. He's been gone for a quarter of an hour now. I hope it helps you. It's the best that can be done at short notice.'

'Good of you,' said the Picaroon. He thanked him and hung up, then stared across at MacNab. 'Information on the way, Mac. From Miller.' He lifted the receiver again and dialled the *Post Courier*. When he got through, 'I'd like to speak to Miss Pennant, please. Yes, at the reception desk.'

She came on a second or two later. 'Anne Pennant speaking.'

'Ludovic Saxon. Whom do you talk to any oftener than me?'

'Has something happened, Mr. Saxon?'

'Not yet,' the Picaroon said. 'I want to ask you one or two more questions. Think about them carefully before you answer.'

'All right. I'll do my best.'

'First,' Ludovic said, 'how often have you been at the Down-Under Club?'

'Three or four times. Four, I think.'

'And each time with your friend, Miss Tarn?'

'Yes. I'm not a member. You have to be a member to go there, unless you're taken by a member.'

'And the members are all Australians or New Zealanders?'

'I couldn't be certain about that. Practically everyone seemed to be.'

'Did you ever see Larry Huth at the club when you were there?'

'Oh, yes. I saw him on several occasions. He was an Australian, you know. I expect he'd go there if there was anything special on just to keep in touch.'

'Did he ever see you there?'

'I expect he would. I mean if I saw him, he'd likely see me.'

'Quite likely,' Ludovic said. 'Now think. Did he ever see you along with this New Zealand boy you mention? Miss Tarn's friend.'

'Rick Stillwell?' She thought for a moment. 'Yes. It's very likely. I was at the club at a party about six weeks ago and Milly was with Ricky. Anyway, there was a phone call for her and she had to go back to her office. She left me with Rick and I was with him for an hour or so, then he took me home.'

Ludovic sighed. 'Then that could explain what Larry Huth said to you, couldn't it? "I saw your boy friend last night." Yes or no?'

She thought about it. 'Yes, it could, Mr. Saxon. I hadn't thought of that because I hadn't thought of Rick like that. He's positively ancient.'

'I know,' the Picaroon said bleakly. 'Thirty.'

'Well, nearly. I mean you begin to rust at twenty-three or so, don't you?'

'It's the way of the world,' Ludovic said. 'Thank you for your help.'

'I don't see that it does help a lot.'

'It helps me,' Ludovic said. 'By the way, which firm does Milly Tarn work for?'

'Maudley and Merrington Fashions.'

'I see, with headquarters in London?'

'In Paris really. Milly is abroad a good deal. That's why I don't see so much of her now.'

'It's a woman's world,' the Picaroon said. He thanked her again and hung up.

MacNab removed the pipe from his mouth. 'What was all that?'

The Picaroon sighed. 'Tidying up, Mac. It puzzled me what Huth meant when he said to the Pennant girl that he had seen her boy friend last night. "Last night" must have meant the night before he disappeared.'

'That's right.'

'So it would be very useful to know where he spent it,' Ludovic said. 'I'm hoping that we'll get that information from Miller's list. It fills out the picture.' He reached for a cigarette. 'My guess is that Huth got a whisper about Donlevy and his crowd and started to follow it up.'

'You think that Donlevy went to this Down-Under Club?'

'Donlevy?' Ludovic shook his head. 'No. I don't imagine for a moment that he did. Donlevy might not be known in England, but there were plenty of Australians who would be familiar with his record and appearance. It would be too dangerous for him to frequent

146

any club where Australians would be likely to gather. Don't forget he'd been a policeman at one time. A fellow like Huth, who'd been on the staff of a newspaper would be familiar with a good many policemen—and especially one who'd turned crook. No, I don't think Donlevy would have looked near this Down-Under Club, but it's likely enough that some of the lesser known members of his crowd might have gone there.'

'That's a fact,' MacNab said. 'Just to keep in touch with things.'

The Picaroon nodded. 'Someone like Millicent Tarn, for example.' He crossed to the table on which the telephone rested, sought the appropriate directory and spent a few minutes searching through it.

'Maudley and Merrington Fashions. Nothing doing.' He leafed over a page or two. 'Not listed. It makes one wonder.'

The bell rang as he spoke.

MacNab went through to the front door. A moment later he returned with a manilla envelope in his big hand. 'The young man from the *Post Courier*. I thought at first he was a young woman.' He handed it over.

The Picaroon opened the envelope. There was a brief covering note from Miller.

This is the best that I can do at the moment. I've made a fairly thorough check and I don't think I've missed out a great deal. Mrs. Huth might be able to help out with a few of the blank nights.

M. M. M.

The Picaroon opened the single sheet and ran his eyes down it with interest. 'There's only one date I'm really interested in now,' he said. 'That's the day before he disappeared.' He stabbed at a line with his forefinger. 'Here we are, Mac. It's working out all right.'

'What does it say?'

'*Huth came in around eleven o'clock. Spoke to Carnegie, the City Editor for a few moments. Worked at his desk for an hour. Lunch at the Press Club. Two of the staff—Finch and Lawson—saw him there as late as three o'clock. At his desk from around four till five-thirty. Left the office along with Quinn at that time. Was seen by Blanche Perrin at the Down-Under Club around nine o'clock at night, talking to a fair girl. Miss Perrin does not know who she was. She did not see him leave but considers he must have done so early as the crowd began to thin out around that time.*'

The Picaroon looked up. 'That's that. He got home all right. He went back to the *Post Courier* next morning, left the building as we know. That was when they must have picked him up.'

There was a little silence.

Ludovic said, 'It's easy enough to see what happened. Huth had stumbled on something which led him to think he was on the track of the bullion robbers. The letter to Millicent Tarn proves that much, and also that he was pushing inquiries in Australia. This brother of hers let her know that Huth was digging and they couldn't have that.'

The doorbell rang as he spoke.

MacNab looked at him significantly. 'Wheat!'

'I've got a feeling you're right,' the Picaroon said grimly.

MacNab walked slowly and deliberately from the room.

23

It was Peter Saltmarsh who came in.

'Found him on the doormat,' said MacNab, with the air of someone who has discovered a strange bug. 'Shivering with the cold, no less. Just you sit in at the fire and get a heat. Peter and I'll make you up a drop toddy. It's not a day for man or beast, but I know what's good for you.' He hurried away on his errand of mercy.

Peter Saltmarsh stretched his legs out towards the fire. 'We've been working on it, Ludovic. Frankly I haven't turned up a great deal. We've checked on Usher, and on Miss Prosser and on Carraccini. I've had a man digging up all he could get on Donlevy and his crowd. There's nothing new in it. What about you?'

'We're on the right road.'

MacNab appeared with a beaker cradled in his hand. 'Just you settle down, Peter, and sup that up. It'll do you no harm at all.'

Saltmarsh accepted it cautiously. 'It looks an awful lot, Mac. About a pint I should say.'

'It's the sugar that makes it look a lot,' MacNab said. He settled in his big armchair and produced a pipe.

Peter Saltmarsh looked across at the Picaroon. 'I'll give you what we've got on them.' He took a notebook from his pocket.

'Carraccini first. Alfred Carraccini—sixty-seven—married with no family. Lives at 368, Childer Road, Acton. Has been with Smail and Usher for twenty-seven years. His hobby seems to be gardening. He's a keen gardener, specialising in roses. No brothers but has one sister, married and living in Swansea. His reputation seems to be sound enough. So far, at least no one has said anything against him. During the war he was in the gunners and picked up a Military Medal. He was wounded in the leg and has a slight limp. He draws a small government pension.'

'Write him off,' Ludovic said.

'I think so,' Saltmarsh agreed. 'Miss Prosser.'

'What have you got on her?'

'Amy Prosser—44. She lives, as I told you before, at 29, Mallow Court, Chelsea. She's been with Usher for roughly about six years now. She is a Canadian.'

'That much we know.'

Saltmarsh nodded. 'Right. I had Darby find out what he could. The neighbours say she's a very quiet woman. She's been living in her present flat for three years now. Before that she was at Kelman Quadrant, Kensington. Originally she came from Toronto. The job with Usher is the first she is known to have had in this country. Usher apparently finds her very efficient and she does most of the I.R. work. That takes her out of town occasionally. Apparently Smail and Usher have got some country clients. Twice in the last three years she has been in Canada for a spell.'

'Interesting,' the Picaroon said.

'She drives a car—a 1967 Riley, a maroon job which she keeps in a lock-up about ten minutes' walk from her flat in premises belonging to a fellow called Furnace. Furnace says she pays well and on the nail. She's kept the car with him for close on six years. She uses it a good bit at weekends. He says she's got a country cottage some place on the South Coast. So far as Darby knows, there are no men in her life at all. There don't seem to be any women either. That's all.'

Ludovic lit a cigarette. 'What about Mally Sheldon?'

'Things seem to be going about all right there. Tempest has been keeping his eyes open, but so far there's been nothing to arouse suspicions.' He took a pull at the beaker he held in his hand. 'You said you were on the right road?'

'That's right,' Ludovic said.

'Then you've got something?'

'I think so,' Ludovic said. 'Listen.' He sat back and spoke quietly and convincingly for the next quarter of an hour and the little man listened in silence. Then, when he had finished, Saltmarsh leaned over.

'And you think you've traced Huth to this house in Berkshire?'

'I'm pretty sure. I'm not certain. If I'd been certain I'd have done something about it. All I needed was a screwdriver. I could have gone back to the car for that. If I'd been really certain I'd have chanced it, but it was one of these problems you have to think about. Was it Huth? If it was, was he in a condition to be removed? Getting him out of the cellar would have been one thing.'

'And you think the Donlevy gang have been using the house as a hide-out?'

'I think the bullion could be hidden there.'

Peter Saltmarsh stared. 'You really think that, Ludovic?'

The Picaroon nodded. 'I think so. Hillmeet is close enough to the scene of the robbery to make it possible.' He crossed to a cabinet, produced a survey map and spread it on the table. 'You've got a network of roads in that part of the country. It would have been possible. My guess is that the Pines had already been purchased by the Donlevy crowd especially for this job.'

Saltmarsh stared at him in silence. 'Everything laid on. Money no object, you might say. They tell me there is threequarters of a million pounds' worth of gold gone amissing. It's a fair amount.'

Ludovic nodded. 'It was well worthwhile. The risks were big—but so was the profit—and they made it quickly. Big money. Quick money—and you have to take big risks.'

Peter laid down his beaker. 'I don't know whether it's

the toddy or what you have to tell me, Ludovic, but my head is going round in circles.'

'It isn't the toddy anyway,' MacNab advised. 'Not for all you had of it.'

Peter Saltmarsh lit a cigarette. 'What happens now?'

Ludovic sighed. 'We're leading up to the crunch, Peter. We're going to need some help. How would you like to be in on it?'

'It's dicey.'

'What would you expect?'

'I could put nine men on the job,' Saltmarsh said thoughtfully, 'including myself. Six of them are married, Ludovic. Five of them have families. The Donlevy gang are killers. We know that from their record. You're asking a lot.'

'You're not answering me.'

'If you're right,' Saltmarsh said, 'I'd say it's a job for the police.'

'Policemen are often married too,' Ludovic said. 'They have families, Peter, just like the rest of you. I'd hate to make a lot of trouble for the police.'

'They couldn't be rushed?'

'Not by daylight.'

'You got in last night. That could happen again.'

'Maybe,' the Picaroon said. 'I shouldn't bet on it. I've got an idea things may be tightening up.' He produced an envelope and ultimately a letter, handing it across to the little man.

Saltmarsh opened it.

31, Southend Park Street,
Sydney.
November 9th

Dear Milly,

I had a word with Outridge a couple of days ago. I met him by accident, but it was a good job I did. He tells me he was in Adelaide . . .

He read through it then looked up. 'Who is this Harvey.'

'From what you can read there, Millicent Tarn's brother.' Ludovic's voice was soft. 'You can see from that what has happened. Huth had learned enough about the bullion robbery to make him interested. He was trying to pick up information in Australia about Millicent Tarn. Note well what he says, Peter. "Reporters with long noses can mean trouble." Huth was one. Maybe they have had their suspicions about him. Whether or not this letter would put them wise.' He smiled grimly. 'You know what happened to him.'

Saltmarsh nodded. 'They've had him for pretty close to two weeks now. If they have got him—if he was the fellow you heard at the Pines, why haven't they got rid of him? It seems the safe thing to do.'

The Picaroon shrugged. 'I can see your point. They put Lockwood down quickly enough when they had to, but don't forget, Lockwood had got away and had something to tell. They had to put him down. And I've got no doubt they'll do the same to Huth when they're ready to do so. I'd say someone wants to see him first— and question him before he goes out.'

'Who?'

'It could be your Mr. Raphael.'

Saltmarsh thought it over. 'I suppose you're right, Ludovic.'

'I think I am. I didn't see Huth. I heard someone. It could have been Huth. If it was, he could well have been drugged.'

The clock chimed two o'clock.

Peter Saltmarsh straightened up. 'Look, I've got to get back to the office.'

'What do you think, Peter? Do you want to come in?'

Saltmarsh looked at him uneasily. 'It isn't a matter of wanting, Ludovic. I've got to think of my operators.

You think you've got the Donlevy gang bottled up. You know their reputation just as well as I do. They've killed before. They'll kill again.'

The Picaroon laughed softly. 'You've made your point, Peter. Suppose Mac and I cope with that angle? Will you be in the background to help out?'

Peter Saltmarsh rose. 'What do you mean?'

The Picaroon told him. He took ten or twelve minutes to do so and at the end of that time the little man sighed

'All right, you've sold me. I'll come myself. I'll bring the single men. That makes four of us.'

'Well done, Peter!' MacNab batted him on the shoulder. 'You do just that, my lad. What is the use of worrying anyway? It never gets you anywhere worth while. The hospitals and asylums is full of folk that got there by worrying. Just you do what you're told and enjoy yourself, and it will be money in your pocket into the bargain.'

Saltmarsh sighed. 'When do you want me to get there?'

'Make it ten o'clock,' Ludovic said. 'Mac will be with you. He'll take charge of matters till I get there. I'm not asking you to make a move at all. All you have to do is keep the place under observation until I get a chance to prove that I'm right about things. If I am, we'll bring in the law.'

'Right,' Saltmarsh said. He swung round. 'I'm getting out of here, Ludovic, before I forget I'm a respectable professional man and get conned into something I can't talk my way out of.' He headed towards the door. When he reached it, he swung round. 'I'll get things organised, Ludovic. I'll ring you when I've got that attended to. One thing more. What about Mrs. Huth? Do you want to tell her anything yet?'

'Not yet. I think I'm right, but I could be wrong. That would be hell for her.'

154

'It would,' Saltmarsh said and took his departure, with MacNab moving ponderously in the rear.

The Picaroon stretched his long legs out towards the fire. He looked up as MacNab reappeared.

'What happens now?' MacNab enquired.

'We make one or two preparations,' the Picaroon said. 'We'll need both cars. You'll get the tanks filled, Mac. Tyres and oil checked. I'll . . .'

The bell rang loudly and peremptorily.

MacNab sat bolt upright. 'What this time! Would you listen to him too! Keeping his finger on the button. Stop you till I give him the length of my tongue frightening the life out of folk like that, as well as spoiling the battery.' Briskly he made for the front door.

24

It was Chief Superintendent Wheat without a doubt. He walked in ahead of MacNab, carrying his large bowler hat in his hand, and when he came into the sitting-room he nodded curtly to the Picaroon. ''Afternoon, Mr. Saxon.'

'Septimus,' said the Picaroon, 'I thought it would be. I recognised your finger on the bell-push. You've got music in your soul, Sep. Get some beer, Mac.'

Superintendent Wheat shook his head. 'No beer.'

'No beer?'

'No beer,' Wheat repeated sternly. 'I'm here on business, Mr. Saxon. I'm not mixing it with pleasure either.'

'There is no pleasure in beer drinking,' MacNab said. 'You might as well talk about pleasure in drinking water. But if you're here you'll just have to take the hospitality of the house.' He made his way out to the kitchen.

Ludovic indicated a chair. 'Make yourself comfortable, Sep.'

For a moment it seemed that Chief Superintendent Wheat would carry his stiffness to the length of standing throughout the interview, then, abruptly, he dropped into an armchair, laid his hat on a little table at his hand and looked at the Picaroon. 'Have you considered what I told you yesterday, Mr. Saxon?'

'I've considered it well, Septimus. I'm considering it at this very moment.'

'And what conclusion have you come to?'

'Here's the beer,' Ludovic said. 'Give it to him, Mac.'

MacNab laid a tray on Wheat's plump knees. 'There you are, Wheat, a bottle of the stuff. Worry away at that. It'll do you good.'

Septimus Wheat would have ignored it, but the tray was not level and it was necessary for him to steady the bottle to prevent it from slipping, and from steadying it to pouring it out was a step so slight that now he did so automatically. He laid it aside without comment, raised the pot to his lips and drank deeply.

Wheat wiped his mouth with a large white handkerchief. 'Right, Mr. Saxon. Have you thought over what I had to say to you yesterday?'

'I've thought of it.'

'I want a statement,' Wheat said. 'We've been looking into this business. Lockwood had been missing from his office for several days now. He hadn't been at his lodgings. He had a bed-sitter at Earls Court. You were round at his office in Gower Lane asking about him. You talked to the young lady at Klein and Weissman's. She described you. No mistake about that. You wanted to know if he had a typewriter. You wanted to know his address. You got it.'

The Picaroon sighed. 'I've been busy.'

'Smart,' MacNab said. 'Getting around.'

Wheat went on impassively, 'You called at Lockwood's place in Pelling Lane. Mrs. Asher described you. You asked her a lot of questions about Lockwood. She took you into his room. She wanted to report his absence to the police. You advised her not to do it. In the end she said she'd wait another twenty-four hours. You also asked her if Lockwood had a typewriter.' His pale blue, bulging eyes peered at Ludovic. 'You're very interested in typewriters, Mr. Saxon. Why?'

'Go on,' Ludovic said.

Wheat nodded. 'I don't need to go on any further. We both know what happened to Lockwood.' His voice went on tonelessly. 'He was shot dead. The bullet that killed him was fired from the same gun that was used to kill two men in the gold robbery. You were at Connelly's the night Lockwood was killed. I can prove that to my own satisfaction. You phoned divisional headquarters and reported a murder.' He sat back and stared in silence.

The Picaroon nodded. 'You make it sound a lot, Septimus.'

'It is a lot. It's enough to make a great deal of trouble for you.'

'You think I had a hand in the gold bullion robbery?'

Wheat shook his head. 'Did I say so, Mr. Saxon? You were in Australia when that happened. Anyway, that kind of killing isn't in your line and I know it better than most. You weren't mixed up in the gold job. That was Donlevy. It was the gun that was used by the Donlevy mob that killed Lockwood. That's what I'm interested in. How much do you know?'

Ludovic reached for the cigarette box. He pushed it across. 'Cigarette, Sep?'

'I'm not interested in cigarettes. I want information. If I don't get it, I've got enough of my own to make things very awkward for you indeed.'

'Very awkward,' the Picaroon said.

Wheat's eyes lit up. 'So you admit it?'

'Not me,' the Picaroon said, 'but you've got me interested, Septimus.' He put his head back and let the smoke drift upwards. 'I've got an idea you and I are going to get together on this business to our mutual advantage.'

Wheat stared at him. 'What do you mean?'

'You know something I know. I know something you know.' Ludovic put his head on one side like an inquiring little bird. 'Swap?'

There was a little silence.

Wheat shook his head. 'I'm not going to do any horse-trading, Mr. Saxon.'

'If you want to get any information from me—that's the only way you are going to get it.'

Wheat's hand went out to the glass.

'More beer,' said the solicitous MacNab. 'It's empty. Just hold you on and I'll get you a drop more.' He left the room abruptly.

Ludovic smiled gently. 'Since there's just you and I, Septimus, with no third party, not even Mac for the moment, let me say you're quite right. I have got information. A lot of information. If I'm right, and I think I am, I can tell you where to put your hands on the Donlevy crowd—and more than the Donlevy crowd—the party who planned it all—Mr. Raphael!'

Wheat had stiffened. 'That's true?'

Lulovic nodded. 'If I'm right. I could be wrong. I give you I'm seldom wrong, but there has to be a first time, Septimus.'

Wheat was breathing very heavily through his thick, white nostrils. 'What about the gold?'

The Picaroon waved an airy hand. 'One is not interested in the—loot. These material considerations, Septimus, do not . . .'

MacNab came back with a fresh bottle and poured it into the glass.

Septimus Wheat sat with his eyes glued to the Picaroon. When he spoke his voice was thick and in his own ears it seemed a long, long distance away. 'If you mean what you say, Mr. Saxon, I'll buy it. I'll buy it if they throw me out on my ear tomorrow.'

'What about your pension?' Ludovic asked interested.

'There's that,' Wheat agreed. 'Well, it isn't all that much of a pension anyway. Right, I'll do a deal with you.'

'Scout's honour.'

There was a harassed expression in Wheat's eyes. 'None of that capering, Mr. Saxon. This is the biggest thing of my career. Donlevy is responsible for four deaths that I know about. I want to get him.'

'We think alike,' Ludovic said. 'Bend over, Wheat. Put your shell-like ear to my lips and listen.'

'Get on with it,' Wheat said irritably.

'It began like this,' Ludovic said. 'A chap called Huth went amissing.' He settled back and spoke briskly and confidently for the next quarter of an hour and Chief Superintendent Wheat was an avid listener.

When he had finished, Wheat leaned forward. 'And you say you know where Huth is being kept a prisoner? You know where the Donlevy crowd are?'

'I think I do.'

Wheat watched him anxiously. 'Where?'

'Secret,' said the Picaroon. 'We'll keep that dark for the moment.'

'This is the truth?'

'Did you ever know me to lie to you?' asked the Picaroon.

Wheat touched his hand to the perspiration which bedewed his forehead. 'Where?' he said again.

Ludovic said briskly, 'You'll have to wait, Septimus. I say I could be wrong. But if I am, it's only in details. I've got the general outline of the business worked out. I've told you enough to let you see that. Give me twenty-four hours to prove I'm right. That's all I ask. Twenty-four hours. By the end of that time I'll have made certain that I'm right. You know what that means. Nothing going wrong at the last moment. No one being tipped off. No suits for false arrests. You get it handed to you on a plate.'

Wheat ran a pink tongue over his dry lips. 'But why?'

'Two reasons,' Ludovic said. 'One—I like to be in at the death. Why should the police have all the fun when Mac and I have done all the work? Two, profit. There's a lot of money involved. There is a very handsome reward posted. I have heard it whispered, Septimus, that the sum is fifty thousand pounds. If there is going to be credit and profit on this one, the credit can go to Septimus Wheat just so long as there is profit for the Picaroon.'

Wheat stared at him in silence.

'Yes or no?'

'Yes.'

'Excellent,' said the Picaroon. 'I've given you what I've got. Now let's empty your basket.'

25

Wheat gave a long, long sigh. 'What do you want?'

'I want to know a little more about this Donlevy gang,' Ludovic said. 'I want to know something about the mysterious Mr. Raphael I hear so much about. These matters of loot and villainy interested me strangely. In such affairs I am a child in arms.'

Wheat looked at him sourly. 'Quite so, Mr. Saxon.'

'In fact,' the Picaroon said, 'we've been out of the country quite a lot in the last couple of years. You cannot expect amateurs and innocents like ourselves to be *au courant*, as you might say, with the criminal scene. Now to get down to it, Septimus. I know you of old. None better. If you've been handling the investigations into the gold robbery, you're the man for my money. I want to know about Donlevy. Speak up.'

Wheat nodded. 'Fair enough, Mr. Saxon. Donlevy is an Australian and an ex-policeman. He was on the force for seven years before they found out he was bent. When they did, they were going to prosecute him and he'd have got ten years, only he slid out before they could get their hands on him.'

'Tip off?'

'So they tell me.'

'How old is he?'

'Forty-two. He's a big, rough chap. Six foot one, weighing in at fourteen stone six. He's a dead shot. So far as we know, he's been responsible for the death of three men as a result of the hold-up—and for Lockwood. That's in England. His reputation in Australia is no better. They've got two deaths chalked up against him there—and two others suspected.'

'And he goes in for big jobs?'

'Yes. There was the Adelaide bank robbery. That was big enough. There was the Keldon-Kleinberg hold-up. That was a gold-mine job. The Australian police gave him the credit for both these jobs. After that he dropped out of the news. They weren't certain whether he'd left Australia or whether he was hiding out. There's plenty of room there for hiding.'

'There is indeed,' Ludovic said, 'but he had left Australia?'

'He had. The first thing we knew about it was when this bullion job was pulled off.'

'How did you know it was Donlevy?'

'We got one of them. Cobber Collins. He's on the Moor now. He didn't talk, but he didn't need to. We knew who we were after and we've been after them ever since. Collins was known to be one of the Donlevy crowd. He'd been with them on the Adelaide bank job. He'd been with them on the Keldon-Kleinberg steal. That gave us our lead. We had an Australian policeman flown over here to give us a bit of help. Inspector Hermon. About all the help he was able to give us was that it was Donlevy's type of job. It had the stamp all over it. That was when we first heard about this Mr. Raphael.'

'And who is he?'

Wheat shrugged. 'According to Hermon, Raphael was the man behind Donlevy. The brains of the outfit. The Australian police didn't know very much about Raphael. All they had ever got was a whisper that was circulating. It was something that came in from the narks, but Hermon swore it was true.'

'And you think it was?'

Wheat nodded. 'I've worked on this one, Mr. Saxon. I've had some good help and I've never been ashamed to ask for it when I needed it. There's no doubt about it at all. Raphael is the man behind these jobs. Raphael is the planner. He's a master of detail. He's worked out the jobs.

'Donlevy is just a hard man. Big, tough and ready to shoot at the drop of a hat. He was the man for carrying out the job, but he couldn't have planned it. That goes for the lot. Kuvelik is just the same. There's one of them —an ex-wrestler called the Blue Parrot. From what we know of him he's an Assyrian—Collins was the same.'

'And the planning is done by Mr. Raphael?'

'There's no doubt about that. Raphael is behind them. Without Raphael the Donlevy crowd would just be another stick-up gang. Bad enough, but no real menace.'

The Picaroon looked thoughtful. 'This Kuvelik?'

'Pole. He's Australian born. He used to be a driver.' Wheat watched the Picaroon unblinkingly. 'Donlevy has hand-picked a lot of useful men, Mr. Saxon.'

'I can see that.'

'A rough collection,' MacNab said soberly.

Ludovic pondered. 'What's Donlevy's background?'

'Fairly straightforward. Irish parents, but he was born in Australia—Perth, we understand. His father was an engineer. According to Hermon he was away from home a lot and Chris Donlevy got out of hand. Not so much, however, that later on he wasn't able to join the police force. He did quite well too. He was a sergeant in the uniform branch. And then he broke loose.'

'Married or single?'

'Married,' Wheat said. 'No family. His wife was a more educated type. Hermon says she was a schoolteacher. She left him while he was still a policeman and she got a divorce.'

'What was her name?'

'Millicent Rigby. Her father was a university professor. He's dead now.'

Ludovic looked at him with respect. 'You've done your homework, Septimus.'

'How else can you get the job done?' Wheat looked at him impassively. 'I'm like every other policeman who tries to do his job. I put all I've got into it. Maybe it isn't such a lot, but I keep on trying. Anyway, that's the ex-Mrs. Donlevy's story. She left Donlevy to go back to live with her father.'

'And divorced Donlevy?'

'Yes. No question about that. Hermon had the details at his fingertips.'

'Where is she now?'

'We don't know. The C.I.B. tried to locate her a year or two back, but her father had died and she couldn't be found. Hermon said there was talk about her going to the States. He thought it might have been California. That's all we've got. Does it help?'

'It fills things out,' Ludovic said pensively.

Wheat looked at the clock then consulted his watch. 'I've got to get back to the office for a conference. I've got to have something to tell them. This story of yours —but I have to know the location of the house.'

'Later.'

'What do you mean by later?'

'Tomorrow.'

Wheat shook his head. 'That won't do, Mr. Saxon. If you're right, we've got to move fast. If Huth is there and alive, we've got to get to him before this crowd put him out of the way.' His voice was stony.

Ludovic thought it over. 'No. It won't work out, Wheat. I'll tell you why. You go back to the Yard with this story and tell it, the matter is out of your hands. I've put a lot of work on this and I've had one astounding stroke of luck.'

'What was that?'

'I'll tell you later,' the Picaroon said. 'No, you've got to do it my way, Septimus. If you report at your conference the matter goes out of your hands—and, what is a good deal worse, my friend, it goes out of mine.'

'What happens then?'

'Listen,' said the Picaroon and told him.

Wheat sat in silence. 'I don't like it, Mr. Saxon.'

'You can learn to like it.'

'You're taking too big a chance.'

'I don't think so. Anyway, you have to take a chance either way. And don't forget I'm the one who's taking the chance. Yes or no?'

For a long moment Septimus Wheat looked at him. 'Yes.'

'Good man,' said the Picaroon. 'I'll get in touch with Saltmarsh and he'll brief you. And remember what I've said, Septimus. Hand-picked men.'

'I'll remember,' Wheat said, and reached for his hat.

Two minutes later, they were alone.

26

It was seven o'clock and sleet rattled on the broad window behind the Picaroon's shoulders. The remains of a meal were still on the table and MacNab, a pipe in his mouth, began to load them on to the trolley. He pushed it through to the kitchen. 'There is just time to wash up. Just you get the hold of a dish towel and we'll tidy this little lot up.'

The Picaroon obliged. He was not domesticated, but in times of dire emergency could always be depended on to accommodate.

MacNab tossed the towel into the dirty linen basket. 'That's that. I'm for off now. I'll pick up Peter and his boys at the office.'

Ludovic nodded. 'Yes, you've got plenty of time. I don't have to be at Becker's till ten o'clock.'

MacNab frowned. 'And you're sure they'll take you to the Pines?'

The Picaroon nodded. 'Where else, Mac? The Pines is their headquarters. The Pines is where they've cached the bullion. The Pines is where they have Huth.'

'If you're right.'

'I can't see how I can be wrong.' He shook his head. 'No—we have to be right here.'

'If you ask me,' MacNab said bluntly, 'Usher is setting you up for something and you're going to get it this night.'

Ludovic nodded. 'Maybe. But this crowd have known I've been in this from the day we stepped into it. They knew Mally Sheldon had engaged Lockwood. My idea is they had her watched—followed her to Lockwood's office in Gower Lane. After that they took Lockwood. My guess is that Lockwood started to work on this job and that they went after him. They got on to Lockwood by following Mally Sheldon. If they followed her to Lockwood's place, they would follow her here and if they did, they would have a pretty good idea why she came. We know they did, because they tried to pick you off with a rifle that very night.'

'It's the truth,' MacNab said. 'The devil's own!'

'So they knew from the beginning that I was in,' Ludovic said, 'but I've got the idea they didn't suspect I was Dyson. If they do suspect, they don't actually know, and they want to find out. My idea is that they couldn't be certain. Usher saw me at his office once, but he didn't want me back again and sent me along to Becker. I'm relying on it that Becker will have had his instructions and that those will be to get me to Hillmeet for a confrontation.'

MacNab shook his head. 'I don't like it at all, at all.'

'I'm looking forward to it.'

166

'And what will you do if they make up their mind to deal with you at Becker's place there without bothering their heads about taking you to Hillmeet? They can do all the confronting they need on the spot.'

Ludovic laughed. He patted his pocket. 'I've got a gun, Mac.' He looked towards the clock. 'Time you were on your way.'

'It is that,' MacNab said and made his way to his room to make his final preparations. It was ten minutes later that he emerged, and when he did so, he was enveloped in an enormous navy duffle coat and wearing a cloth cap. He patted his pocket carefully. 'I've got everything. Good luck to you and just you watch yourself. One of these days you'll stick your neck out too far.'

The Picaroon sighed. 'If I go to Hillmeet, you'll be there and so will Peter and his boys. If they've got some other plan in mind, well, I've had to deal with that sort of thing often enough before.' He let MacNab out, went along to the cloak-room and drew on a trench coat. He left the lights lit in the sitting-room and let himself out by way of the door at the rear of the garage. A door in the high stone wall at the rear of the premises opened into the alley. He stepped into this and turning the key in the lock, dropped it into his pocket.

Ten minutes walking took him to Lyman's Hotel. He made his way up to the room on the fourth floor, opened the door of the wardrobe and lifted out the clothing that Tod Dyson assumed. He changed now, sat down in front of the mirror and went to work on his features.

It was close on twenty minutes later that he left the hotel and made his way to the underground. There was a gun in his pocket, a flat, blue-black Belgian automatic, and there was a cosh in his pocket. When he reached the bottom end of Prior Lane he went into a telephone kiosk, laid a handful of change on the little metal tray and produced a notebook.

There were four telephone numbers in it, and the first

was that of Simon Usher's house at Golders Green. He dialled the number and waited.

It was a man's voice who answered him.

The Picaroon said, 'May I speak to Mr. Usher, please?'

'Mr. Usher is not at home, sir.'

'Who is speaking?'

'Martindale, sir. I have been with Mr. Usher for several years. May I have your name, sir?'

'Dyson,' the Picaroon said. 'Tod Dyson.'

'Thank you, sir. I shall let Mr. Usher know you have called when he returns.'

The Picaroon considered. Was it possible that the enterprising Mr. Usher was still at his desk at this hour of night? He dialled Smail and Usher, but there was no response and after a moment or so, he hung up and rang Miss Prosser's flat in Chelsea.

Again the telephone rang with the dreary sound of a telephone ringing in an empty flat. He listened to it for a moment or so, then hung up and glanced at his watch.

Four minutes to ten.

He dialled Millicent Tarn's flat in Rennick Road.

No answer.

The Picaroon laughed softly, laid down the receiver and opened the heavy door. A gust of wind tossed a handful of sleet at him. He turned up the collar of his coat, drew down the brim of his hat and walked along to 111 Prior Lane. He halted outside the entrance and looked around him.

Six cars parked in the short street. So far as he could see, they were all empty. When he looked up at the front of the building, he saw that the blinds of Becker's windows had been drawn, but that round the edges of them was a thin rim of yellow light.

He went along towards the stairs, dipped his hand into his pocket and felt the butt of the gun. He halted there for a moment, listening attentively, but there was neither sign nor sound of movement.

He went upstairs quietly, halting on each landing to listen for a moment before proceeding to the next, but still there was no sound to alert him. He moved along silently until he reached the door of Becker's room and here he halted again. For the space of two minutes he remained there, but the building was silent and still. With gentle fingers he tried the handle. It opened and he stepped inside, closing the door behind him.

The ante-room was empty. No Elke. But would Becker have Elke on the premises tonight? The Picaroon doubted that. He stood there looking around him. The room was lit by a single light suspended from a drop cord. The chair had been pushed into one corner, but the ashtrays were piled with cigarette ends, and the room reeked of stale smoke.

Ludovic moved forward quietly. He reached the inner door, turned the handle and opened it very gently, pushing it right back to the wall.

Harry Becker was waiting for him at his desk. He lay with his head on the blotter which had absorbed a good deal of the blood which had seeped from the hole above his right temple.

The Picaroon smiled wryly. The engaging Mr. Raphael had decided to tidy up!

He stepped backwards, closing the door as he did so, crossed the floor of the ante-room and, pushing it open, looked out.

The corridor was deserted.

He stepped into it closing the door of Becker & Knightly behind him. Again he stood to listen, but the building was still silent and still. He walked quickly along towards the stairs. He had all but reached them when he heard the intake of breath as the cosh swung at him.

In a flash he had swivelled round. He was vaguely aware that another door stood open, and that two men had waited for him in the premises of Hurst & Tyndal, when the first blow took him and brought him to his knees.

He grabbed for the automatic and his fingers had tightened over the butt when the second blow landed. There was a third, and the Picaroon slid forward on to his face and lay very, very still.

The man who had used the cosh stood over him for a second or two, breathing heavily. He nodded to his bulky companion. 'All right, Hassan, pick him up. I'll go first and bring the car to the entrance.' He went downstairs quickly.

A moment or two passed. There was the sound of a car starting up and then it began to move forward.

The Blue Parrot lifted the Picaroon in his arms and went downstairs and out to the street.

27

The car was travelling at a steady fifty on a road on which there was but little traffic. The long pathway of light sliced through the darkness and from time to time, the Picaroon saw a clump of trees, a village and a church. Sometimes it was a single light from an isolated cottage.

He sat between two large men in the rear of the car, and one of the large men was of impressive dimensions indeed. As large as MacNab, the Picaroon thought, but not so hard. There was more fat about him, but it was still solid fat. He had been conscious for an hour now, and his hands were looped together with a length of hard, knotted cord. By experiment, he decided that there was about six inches of cord between his wrists. It was sticky in places with the blood that dropped from his head. The cut was above his right ear and the wound had closed up, and clotted now. At the same time he felt oddly weak and dizzy. He moved his hands together up towards his head and the man on his left said: 'Take it easy, chum.'

The man on his left hand had been addressed as Len. The big man on his right was Hassan. The driver had been addressed as Van.

The Picaroon sorted them all out in his mind as it began to clear. Len was Kuvelik, the Polish-Australian. Hassan was the Assyrian wrestler, the Blue Parrot. Van remained Van. He was still thinking it out like that when the headlamps picked out trees on the right some distance away, and the car began to slow down. It made a careful turn to the right and the Picaroon recognised the scene of his accident.

Five minutes later they had reached the house and he had been hustled inside by Kuvelik and the Blue Parrot. In a half-curious fashion he began to wonder why the big man had been called that. He was still wondering about it when he was led into the study.

There were two men there. One of them was a tall square, solidly built man with a tanned face and curiously cold eyes. He sat at one side of the fireplace smoking a cigarette. The other was small, slight, but with a willowy toughness about him.

Kuvelik closed the door. He swung round and said, 'O.K., Chris. We got him.'

The squarely built man threw his cigarette into the fire. 'I'm Donlevy.'

Ludovic nodded. 'I thought so.'

Donlevy was looking him over almost curiously. 'Heard a bit about you, Saxon.'

'That's mutual.'

Donlevy looked at him, grinning, but there was little

mirth in his grin. 'Yes.' He looked back towards Kuvelik. 'Any trouble, Len?'

'No. He walked into it.'

'What about Becker?'

'Dead.'

Donlevy said dryly, 'He's better dead.' He looked towards the Blue Parrot. 'Take him along to the bathroom
and get him tidied up.'

The big man gripped Ludovic by the upper arm. 'This
way.' He led him out and along the hall towards the
stairway. They went up and Ludovic felt himself totter
just a little. When he got to the top floor, he looked along
the hall and saw a tall vase on top of a pedestal, and saw
there were two vases and two pedestals.

Ludovic said thickly, 'How many vases are there on
that stand, Hassan?'

'One,' Hassan said. 'One vase, one stand.'

'I make it two of them,' Ludovic said.

'Double vision,' the Blue Parrot said. 'Concussion.
That is from the cosh. Kuvelik hits hard, eh?'

'Yes.'

'So you be pleased it is not me,' Hassan said. 'I hit lots
harder.' He laughed aloud, pushed open the door of the
bathroom and led the Picaroon across to the wash-basin.
He pointed to a chair by the end of the bath. 'Sit
down.'

Ludovic sat down. He was glad to sit down again and
when he was sitting down the spell of dizziness began
to pass. He watched Hassan run hot water into the wash-
basin, produce a box of cotton wool and a strip of
medicated gauze. He watched the big man upend a bottle
of disinfectant of some sort into the hot water, stir it
around then dip a swab in it.

He went to work on the Picaroon's head with deft
fingers. When he had finished, he pointed to the bowl.
'Your hands. Wash them there.'

Ludovic went across to the basin and dabbed them in

the hot water. When he had finished, Hassan dried them roughly. 'How you feel now?'

'Not so good.'

The Blue Parrot nodded. 'So. It matters very little.' He picked up an aspirin bottle and shook out two, handed them to the Picaroon. He filled a glass with cold water and held it to Ludovic's lips.

The Picaroon drank it all.

Hassan laid down the glass. 'Good. Now we go back.' His big hand gripped Ludovic by his left bicep. 'This way. I tell you something. You try to get away, I break your neck now instead of an hour from now, yes?'

'No,' said the Picaroon.

Hassan laughed. 'You got sense all right.' He laughed heartily. 'This way. We go see what happens now.' At the door of the study, he reached forward, turned the handle and pushed.

Ludovic staggered inside. He shook his head then straightened up.

It was the same room, but the cast had altered a little. The thin man had gone. Donlevy sat at one side of the fire and at the other was Kuvelik.

It was at the desk that he stared now and at the slim, attractive figure who sat there. She was fair and might have been in her early thirties. She wore her blonde hair rather long so that it fell over her shoulders. She wore a smartly cut suit of navy blue with something white at the collar, and she was looking at him with a curious intensity.

The Picaroon sighed. 'The efficient Miss Prosser.'

She laughed softly. 'You recognise me?'

Ludovic nodded. 'How is our mutual friend Mr. Simon Usher faring without your services?'

She smiled at him. 'Mr. Usher won't need me any more.' She looked round. 'Tell him, Chris.'

'Like Becker,' Donlevy said briefly.

173

The Picaroon nodded. 'I see. Tidying up.'

'Yeah.'

'I thought so,' Ludovic said. 'I tried to get hold of him tonight.'

Donlevy put the cigarette back in his mouth.

The girl spoke, almost sharply. 'You tried to phone him?'

'Yes.'

'Why was that?'

'Just like you,' Ludovic said. 'Tidying up. That's the kind of mind I've got. I rang him at his house, I rang him at his office, I also rang you.'

She looked surprised. 'You did?'

'I did,' the Picaroon said. 'One likes to be thorough. When I got no response from Miss Amy Prosser at Mallow Court, I tried Miss Milly Tarn at Rennick Road.'

The room was suddenly silent.

The atmosphere had changed. Ludovic saw Donlevy's harsh features harden. The chair was pushed aside. Donlevy came up from it fast for a big man. He gripped Ludovic by the lapels and jerked him forward. 'Damn you, Saxon! I . . .'

Millicent Tarn said, 'All right, Chris. I'll handle this.'

Donlevy relaxed his grip. He pushed Ludovic back with one big hand. 'Right, Saxon. You wonder why you're here at all. I'll tell you. You're here to talk. If it hadn't been that we wanted to squeeze all we can get out of you, you would be lying on the floor beside Becker right now.'

'I believe it,' Ludovic said. He shook his head to clear away some of the dizziness. He raised both hands to his forehead and held them there for a moment.

Donlevy stood in front of him, watching for a moment, then went back to his chair.

Millicent Tarn was watching him. 'How do you feel '

'Not so good.'

'The cosh,' Hassan said in explanation. 'He has the double vision.'

She smiled at the big man. 'Get him some coffee, Hassan.'

'Sure,' he said. He went out.

She looked over at Donlevy. 'Give him a chair, Chris. If we want to get anything out of him, we'll have to treat him a little better than you've done so far.'

Donlevy crossed the room, picked up a chair and brought it back. He watched the Picaroon sit down, then produced a packet of cigarettes. 'Smoke?'

'Please.'

Donlevy lit one from the one at his own lips, pushed it between the Picaroon's and went back to his chair.

Ludovic said, 'Thanks. Nice of you.'

Millicent Tarn was watching him. 'All right, Mr. Saxon, we'll get on with the questioning.' She watched him for a moment. 'You know what's going to happen to you, don't you?'

'I've got a pretty good idea. To me and to Huth.'

Her eyes flickered.

'Where is he?' Ludovic asked.

She stared at him for a moment. 'There's no reason why you shouldn't know. He's down below. He had a rather unfortunate accident. Hassan used the cosh on him, and Hassan is very strong. We have been wondering what to do about him. We need to talk to him very much to find out just how much he knows—and where he picked up his information. He has been unconscious for several days now—but we kept hoping he would recover.'

'Enough to speak anyway,' Donlevy said.

She nodded. 'Enough to speak. But perhaps you will do.' She lit a cigarette for herself, and as she did so, Hassan came into the room.

He carried a tray in one large hand and on it was

balanced a beaker. He brought it across and the Picaroon brought both hands forward to lift it.

Donlevy leaned towards it. 'Watch it, Saxon. You even look like you're thinking about tossing that mug at anyone and I'll cut your hand off at the wrist. That's a promise.'

'I believe you,' Ludovic said. He did. This man was flint hard. He raised the beaker to his lips and drank some of it. The coffee was hot and it was good. He felt the warm glow of it reach his stomach and strengthen and invigorate him. He sat there, sipping it, savouring it, relishing the sharp astringent bite of it until it was finished.

Hassan came across and relieved him of the empty beaker.

'Now,' the woman said. 'One or two questions, Mr. Saxon. Only one or two, but I want answers from you. And first of all, why did you try to pass yourself off on Usher as Dyson?'

Ludovic shrugged. 'One has to begin somewhere. I didn't know what was behind Huth's disappearance, but when Lockwood went absent I discovered he had paid a visit to Harry Becker.'

Donlevy swore softly.

'I went there too,' Ludovic said simply. 'He put me on to Usher. Harry was a mistake. You should have picked a better man.'

'And then?'

Ludovic shrugged. 'When luck is running my way, I push it. I thought Usher might be able to put something Tod Dyson's way. I was wrong.'

She shook her head. 'No—I met you. I spoke to you. You deceived me. All that was wrong was that we couldn't take a chance. You could have been the man you claimed to be. You could have been a police undercover man. You happened to be Ludovic Saxon.'

There was a little silence.

Donlevy's harsh voice broke it. 'O.K. Where does the Donlevy gang come into it?'

The Picaroon looked round. 'You killed Lockwood. You used the gun that was used on the bullion hold-up.'

Donlevy's head jerked up.

Millicent Tarn was staring at him. 'Chris! You didn't get rid of it!'

He swung round towards her. 'Hell, I . . .'

'You didn't,' she said. 'You kept it and it could have put you away for life. It could have put all of us away.'

'That's it,' Ludovic said. 'The police knew I'd been at Connelly's on the night that Lockwood was murdered. They came round to see me. Superintendent Wheat told me that the bullet had been identified.'

Kuvelik said softly, 'Not so smart, Chris.'

'O.K.,' Donlevy said, 'so we all slip up at times. Hassan puts Huth out so he's no damn use to us. I make a fumble myself. So does this pigeon.' He looked at the woman behind the desk. 'Anything more?'

She nodded. 'How did you find out my identity, Mr. Saxon?'

Ludovic shrugged. 'Bit of luck.'

'Not for you.'

'Not for you, either,' Ludovic said. He rose as he spoke.

Donlevy watched him closely. 'Stand in the one spot, Saxon. Don't try anything.'

'Cramp!' Ludovic said. He limped away from the desk, straightened out his leg, then limped back towards them again. He turned and moved away, this time towards the tall cabinet.

Millicent Tarn was watching him. 'You haven't told me much, Mr. Saxon.'

The Picaroon halted, his shoulders touching the dark, ugly wood. 'It's simpler than you know, Mr. Raphael.'

The room was suddenly silent.

Millicent Tarn said quietly, 'You know that too?'

Ludovic nodded. 'It wasn't so hard to come to that

conclusion. One puts this and that together.' He looked towards the big figure of Donlevy. 'The police were pretty certain that Donlevy hadn't planned his own jobs. The police are a bit smarter than most people give them credit for, and Donlevy had been one of them. The whisper was that there was a brain behind the Donlevy mob— this Mr. Raphael. It had to be true.'

'So you deduced that I was Mr. Raphael?'

The Picaroon sighed. 'It wasn't so much a matter of deduction as luck again. I heard you'd left Donlevy. I'd heard you were a clean woman. I'd heard you were divorced.' He kept on looking at her and an impish little smile came into his eyes. 'This talk about Mr. Raphael puzzled me and I don't like to be puzzled.'

Donlevy was still on his feet. He said, 'O.K., Milly, you've had all you need. When you have to do a thing, you do it quick. That's the way I work it.'

She smiled. 'Always impulsive, Chris.' She shook her head. 'I want to find out where I slipped up, Chris. Mr. Saxon got through to me. What Mr. Saxon did once someone else could do again.' She looked across at the Picaroon. 'I like to learn from my mistakes, Mr. Saxon. I made one, didn't I?'

The Picaroon nodded. 'You could say that.'

'And you're going to tell me about it?'

'Suppose we do a bit of horse-trading?'

Donlevy said, 'Suppose we do a bit of tidying up, Milly. This guy Saxon talks too much. I want to get to bed. So we dig a hole.'

She laughed. 'I don't think it will take long, Chris. What do you say, Len?'

Kuvelik shrugged. 'I'm easy. At the same time I'm kind of interested.'

Millicent Tarn looked across at the Picaroon. 'All right, Mr. Saxon. Something we want to know—something you want to know . . . Ask your question.'

The Picaroon leaned back nonchalantly against the

cabinet, his looped hands in front of him. 'Right. What happened to Lockwood?'

The clock began ticking as he spoke.

Donlevy looked over at it. 'Five minutes you've got, chum.' He took a gun from his pocket and laid it on the desk at his hand.

'Tell me,' Ludovic said. He smiled a ghostly smile. 'I don't care how long you spin it out, Donlevy.'

Donlevy looked at Kuvelik. 'Tell him, Len.'

Kuvelik turned his long, sallow, horse-like face towards the Picaroon. 'Nothing to it, chum. We followed the Sheldon girl to Lockwood's. We knew what she was after. She wanted Lockwood to find Huth.

'O.K. Van and I kept with him all day. He led us around quite a bit, this chum, and that night we followed him back to this dump in Gower Lane and picked him up.'

'I see.'

Kuvelik shrugged. 'We have a little place in Canning Town we use from time to time. We took Lockwood there and had a little talk with him, see? What to do? You don't want dead men all over the place if you can help, so Van and Hassan and I throw a scare into him. Tell him we could put him down for this one and let him think it over.' He smiled a thin smile at Ludovic. 'It don't take him too long to make up his mind about what he wants to do. Which is to get the hell out of it all in one piece.'

'I don't blame him,' Ludovic said.

'Me neither.' Kuvelik's grin widened. 'So we digs up the typewriter and he thumps out a letter to Huth's wife, and we say he stays wrapped up for a day or two till we see what comes out of it.'

Ludovic nodded. 'And then he managed to escape?'

'That's it,' Kuvelik said. 'He clouts Van when he comes in with some tucker for him and is out on the sreets legging it like hell.'

'And one of you got after him?'

'Me. In the green van,' Kuvelik said. 'I had to leave it at a subway station and tail him and I followed him to this Connelly's woodyard, where he holed up.' He looked across at Donlevy. 'I phoned Chris, but he wasn't here at the time. He was over in Ireland. For damn near two whole days we watched this Connelly's dump, and we figure he's still holing up, which he was.' He looked across at Donlevy. 'So Chris comes back to take charge. Tell him, Chris.'

Donlevy said dryly, 'Short and sweet. I went in there and shot him, which is just as well. He turned out to be a sailor I met once or twice when I was a cop.' He scowled at Ludovic. 'That's all.'

The Picaroon sighed. 'I thought it would be like that.'

There was a little silence. Ludovic wondered just how close at hand MacNab and Peter Saltmarsh's men would be. He wondered if Wheat had carried out his own part of the arrangement. He wondered if Kuvelik or Hassan or any of the rest of them did any cleaning or dusting around here. He didn't think it likely, so he did have one chance if he could work it. If he could work it and had a bit of luck.

Millicent Tarn was looking towards him. 'Satisfied?'

'Yes. I thought it would be something like that. I saw the letter Lockwood sent to Mrs. Huth. I had the idea he'd been forced to write it. I didn't think an old sailor would have been so easily discouraged.'

Donlevy's clipped voice said, 'O.K., Milly. Time is running out. All this hanging around don't interest me.'

She looked back at Ludovic. 'Your turn, Mr. Saxon.'

The Picaroon stretched a little, raising his arm just a fraction. 'Right. I started with a pretty big advantage, Miss Tarn—because we'd met before.'

'We had?' She was staring at him, frowning. 'You mean at Smail and Usher's? You mean as Tod Dyson?'

The Picaroon laughed aloud. 'No. A long time before

that. Do you remember an occasion, more than two years ago now when you had a flat tyre outside Reading?'

She had stiffened. 'Outside Reading?'

'East of it—on a little minor road,' Ludovic explained. 'Two pleasant gentlemen changed it for you. You were quite informative. You told me you didn't know very much about changing tyres. You also said you were a nervous driver and that you had once had a bad crash. Of course you had. You received a head injury. You were bare-headed at the time, and I could see the marks of the stitching at your hair-line.'

She was breathing very heavily. 'Yes. My scalp had been cut away.' She laughed suddenly. 'Of course. It was all so simple, wasn't it? I was Amy Prosser on that occasion.'

'That's right,' Ludovic said. 'And when Tod Dyson called at Smail and Usher's he recognised you at once. You claimed to be a Canadian, but it was easy enough to recognise an Australian accent.' He kept on smiling, but at the same time his eyes were circling the room.

Millicent Tarn at the desk, Donlevy close beside it. Four feet and no more. Kuvelik sitting by the fireside and the vast Hassan standing with his broad shoulders against the door.

'So,' he said, 'it worked out. Lockwood had put me on to the Donlevy crowd. The murder made certain and it wasn't so hard to go on from there. The Donlevy crowd were Australians. Huth was an Australian. Amy Prosser was an Australian and when a kind friend mentioned Milly Tarn and I investigated things, I discovered Milly Tarn had been looking around for a secluded country property in Hampshire, several months before the gold steal. It made me think, old girl. In the end you didn't decide on the place in Hampshire. You picked this place. The Pines, Hillmeet, Berks—and it worked out jolly well I'd say.'

There was a little silence.

She laughed. 'It did.'

'Huth is here. The gold is here! And . . .'

There was a sudden smashing of glass from below!

Donlevy took one step towards the gun, then:

'Don't move!'

The Australian swung round.

There was a gun in the Picaroon's hand. He held them both up together. Donlevy snatched at the gun on the desk. He had his fingers on it, when:

Crack!

The bullet tore through his wrist. The gun dropped to the floor at his feet and he stood staring in mute astonishment.

Hassan was on the run. He came charging across like a bull.

The Picaroon shot him in the right shoulder.

The big man spun backwards, then came on again.

Ludovic shot him in the knee.

Hassan staggered forward and fell on his face. His big hand clawed at the bare boards.

Kuvelik sat quite still.

There was the sound of running footsteps close at hand. The shrill note of a police whistle. Someone fired a shot. Another, then there was a scream.

Donlevy tottered forward. 'Damn you, Saxon!'

The Picaroon raised the gun just a little higher. When he spoke his voice was like ice. 'One step, Donlevy, and you get it in the stomach!'

Donlevy drew up.

The sound of running feet was close now. The door crashed open and MacNab's massive figure burst into the room. Behind him were blue uniforms and in a moment it was all over.

Chief Superintendent Wheat appeared a moment later, a jubilant man. He wore his hat very straight on his head.

It was the first time Ludovic had ever seen him with it on indoors. 'You all right, Mr. Saxon?'

'In the pink.' Ludovic was rubbing his wrists. He pointed. 'Introductions. Chief Superintendent Wheat. The lady is Millicent Tarn—the former Mrs. Donlevy. They were divorced, Septimus, but of course, they could have re-married. The divorce would be a blind. Ask her.'

Wheat looked very impersonal. 'Is it so, ma'am?'

She nodded. Her eyes went to the Picaroon. 'That gun. Where did it come from? You were searched before they brought you here.'

Ludovic nodded. 'I was indeed, Millicent, old girl.'

'We took a gun off him,' Kuvelik said hoarsely. 'I'll swear he had nothing on him when . . .'

The Picaroon sighed. 'I used to be a boy scout, Kuvelik. You know our motto. "Be Prepared." I've never forgotten it. I paid a visit here. Last night, in fact. I had an idea things were going to work out something like this, and if they were, it would certainly take place in this room, because it was the only one decently furnished. I know. I looked 'em over. The gun was here. I left it on top of the cabinet. What worried me was getting it down.'

There was a little silence.

Ludovic said, 'My guess is you'll find the gold in the cellars. You'll find Huth there too. He's a badly injured man, and you'd better get him to hospital without delay.' He moved towards the door. 'Mac, what I could do with now is a spot of your water of life. Is it possible that you have a flask handy?'

'It's in my pocket,' MacNab said, and produced it.

The Picaroon upended it. There was a cheerful little gurgle. Through it, he could hear the impersonal voice of Septimus Wheat saying:

'Christopher Donlevy, I have here a warrant for your arrest on a charge of the murder of . . .'

The Picaroon handed back the flask. 'When they get out of here I want to get on to that phone. We've got some good news for Mally Sheldon.'

'It's a God's truth,' MacNab said. He crossed towards the desk, and drew it across towards them.